# A Girl of Two Worlds

# A Girl of Two Worlds

## Lorna Eglin

**CF4·K**

© Copyright 2003 Lorna Eglin
ISBN 978-1-85792-839-6
Reprinted 2014

Published by
Christian Focus Publications,
Geanies House, Fearn, Tain, Ross-shire,
IV20 1TW, Scotland, U.K.
www.christianfocus.com
email: info@christianfocus.com

Cover design by Alister MacInnes
Cover illustration by Rachael Phillips
Inside illustrations by Stuart Mingham

Printed and bound in Denmark
by Nørhaven

AIM International,
3 Halifax Place, Nottingham, NG1 1QN
www.aimint.org/eu

# Contents

# *Introducing Nosim*

Out on the wide plains of Southern Kenya, loved by tourists for its wealth of game and glimpses of majestic Kilimanjaro, live the Maasai people. This little book is the story of a daughter of this fine, free race – a girl born into the age-old customs of her people – a girl born into modern Kenya, with education, progress and change.

It is not a true story of one particular girl. Yet it is a true story. Hundreds of girls from the villages have been brought to the Mission boarding school. Every incident in the book is from the experience of some girl we have known in the ten years of the school's life. 'Nosim' is a pet name mothers use in singing lullabies to their little girls. 'Ng'oto Ntoyie' could be any of the missionary teachers who have cared for these girls through the years. Maasai women are always called Mother of the eldest child. They are puzzled as to what to call the white woman who suddenly became mother of dozens of little Maasai girls. Mother of the Girls – Ng'oto Ntoyie – was the name they coined for her.

Many of the 'Nosims' have gone on in High School, Teacher Training, Nursing, Bible School – they need your prayers in all the temptations and dangers of the New World. Many others have been taken back into the Old World. Pray that even there the Word planted in their hearts may be kept alive. If all who read this little book would lift up their hearts and pray for these Maasai girls, then the future may see many Christian wives and mothers living for the glory of our Master here in Maasailand.

# Her First World

Nosim felt sleepy in the warm silence of the afternoon. The dry dust tickled as it trickled between her bare toes. The sun was hot on her back but the breeze cooled as it played lazily with her 'karash' – the small square of cloth she wore knotted over one shoulder. The yellow grass was rustling restfully around her and the occasional far-off tinkle of a cowbell reminded her that she was not alone under this vast blue sky, with its white worlds of cloud.

Down the slope in front of her, her father's great herd of sturdy, stunted cattle were wandering slowly down to the water-hole. There her brothers, great lordly creatures of ten and twelve summers respectively, were directing the herd with skill and swaggering confidence as the cattle drank thirstily, knee-deep in mud in the dwindling pool.

Presently, feeling hungry, she got up and strolled down the slope towards her brothers. To a little girl who had just lost her front baby-teeth it seemed a long time since the drink of milk in her mother's warm smoky hut that morning. It was still several hours till the sun would be making those long shadows which would tell them it was time to take the cattle home. It was not the custom to take food with them but sometimes the day seemed long to one as small as Nosim. Maybe her brothers, Taki and Tombo, felt hungry too but they would never confess such weakness to a mere girl.

'I'm hungry,' announced Nosim with just the right amount of pleading and confidence that would flatter these male lords. They were kind to their little sister in a condescending way, providing she played her destined role of admiring female faithfully.

'*Wou,*' (come) called Taki as he beckoned her, curling his fingers under the palm of his hand in the accepted way. He caught a cow for her and held it while she scrambled down to where he was, crouched under the thin animal and milked the warm sweet milk straight into her mouth.

Then she got up and wandered off. She did not thank him. One does not thank a superior for a gift. Nor was it necessary for him to warn her not to tell Father about the stolen milk – she knew and could be trusted.

The cattle all watered, the boys started playing. Nosim did not presume to join them. She watched for a while as they challenged each other to ride the biggest and most restless of the herd. They took their falls manfully. Presently she wandered off to pick 'ilamuriak' – the small black berries on the thorny bushes near the water-hole. She collected the blackest, juiciest ones and tied them in the corner of her cloth to take home to her mother. Soon her fingers and mouth were stained and sticky, and her arms and legs scratched from the prickly bushes.

As she wandered on she spied, high up on the trunk of the umbrella thorn tree near her, a hardened trickle of gleaming, golden gum. No Maasai child could resist the hours of delicious chewing which that would give. Without hesitation she scrambled up the tree. The branches were thorny and brittle and the bark dry and crumbly, but Nosim was used to climbing trees. Besides, if she called her brothers to get the gum, her share would be very small. At last she was there and prising the precious sticky lump from the wound in the side of the tree. She called out in triumph to her brothers, popped the sticky lump into her mouth and waved gaily as they spotted her high up in the tree.

Then it happened… With a loud snap the branch on which she was standing broke! She reached out wildly for another but it came away in her hands and she went slithering down, crashing through the thorny branches and on to the hard ground below.

In next to no time her brothers were picking her up and making a fuss and comforting her in a most satisfactory way, for, although they naturally looked down on her for being a mere girl, they were fond of her. Also they were well aware that Father would hold them responsible for any harm that might come to her while they were out together with the cattle. But all the dusting down and clumsy reassurances did not dry her tears this time. She felt cold and the pain in her arm made everything turn round in front of her eyes.

'*Nini, Nini,* (Mummy)' she cried, and when the boys saw her arm they decided to get her back to her mother as soon as possible. Taki set off at a trot along the little winding path back to the village. Nosim, sobbing, wailing and holding her painful arm, ran stumbling behind him.

'*Nini!*' she wailed again loudly as they entered the village and made for Mother's hut. Soon Mother was hurrying out with loving concern and everyone was crowding round.

'The bone is broken,' they pronounced as they heard the story of what had happened from Taki and saw how bent her little arm was. Mother led her off to the shade next to their house and sat down on the cow-skin spread there. She gathered Nosim on to her lap and rocked and comforted her, singing to her and petting her. Nosim relaxed against her hot  ochre-greased skin and nuzzled at the withered breast for comfort. Presently her sobbing stopped but the ache in her arm remained and she felt miserable.

'Menye Sinet will come soon,' reported Taki. He had been sent by his mother to call the old man in a nearby village who was skilled at dealing with broken bones. Father would pay him a goat but he would pay it gladly because it was not everyone who could set bones well. It would cost another goat too. That would be slaughtered and the meat boiled to make nourishing 'motori,' or soup, for Nosim so that she would soon be well and strong again.

Presently Menye Sinet arrived and, at sight of him, Nosim's screaming started all over again. She buried her face in the warm, smelly, familiar cloth under which she had hidden so often when she was a baby. After solemn greetings all round Menye Sinet squatted down next to the screaming Nosim and took her arm gently in his hands. He felt around skilfully with exploring fingers and then, suddenly, just when she was beginning to feel reassured that he would not hurt her, he took her arm more firmly and pulled and twisted it smartly. She screamed with pain and fright but he held it firmly in place. Then he beckoned to a woman standing nearby and she handed him a small soft square of fresh cow-skin.

He wrapped it gently but firmly round Nosim's throbbing wrist, adjusted it and held it in place just where he wanted it. The woman was fumbling in a little tin for her 'oltidu' – a sharpened piece of iron set in a stick for a handle. This found, she also pulled out a piece of thread made from the long sinews in the back of the cow that had been slaughtered last time the village had a celebration. With these she skilfully sewed the edges of the skin together, deftly making holes with her 'oltidu' and then poking the thread through and pulling it tight.

The operation over, Nosim started feeling quite important. Everyone made a fuss over her, coming to see her arm and asking how it had happened. Menye Sinet instructed her mother to take care of the arm for a day or two till the skin hardened and assured her that soon she would feel no pain.

By the next day the skin was getting hard and stiff round her arm. By the second day it was so tight and supported her arm so well that she felt no more pain and was not afraid to move it. Now she settled down to enjoy the petting. Nosim lay in bed in the mornings while the other girls in the village got up before sunrise to help their mothers with the milking. Nosim sat in the shade later in the morning when the other girls were collecting the fresh, steaming cow-dung and helping their mothers smear it on the houses to make them more rainproof, in anticipation of the

rain they were hoping for soon. When mothers and big sisters went off with their large tins to the water-hole many miles away, or took their big knives in the endless search for fire-wood, Nosim was not even given a baby to look after – she just sat with 'Kokoo,' her wizened grandmother who was now too old for work.

Kokoo might be too old for work but she was not too old to tell stories, wonderful stories of the great days of the proud Maasai people and of the far-off Beginnings of the World.

# How her First World Began

'The Moon, my child,' explained Kokoo one evening as they sat and watched the glory of the full Moon rising, 'that beautiful Moon you see there is the wife of the Sun, and their village is the great circle of the Sky. Once, long, long ago, they quarrelled. The Sun struck the Moon and the Moon hit back. It was a terrible fight. When the fight was over and the Sun saw that his face was badly battered, he was ashamed to let anyone see that his wife had struck him. In order to hide this from the people of the world who look up to the Sun each day, he turned on a very bright light. This bright light dazzles our eyes and we cannot see that his face is battered. But the Moon is not ashamed to let people see. Her face is bruised and swollen, her mouth is crooked and one of her eyes is missing as a result of the Sun's awful blows.

'The Sun and Moon are always travelling. They never rest. But sometimes the Moon gets tired and then the Sun catches up with her and carries her for two days. During that time we do not see the Moon at all. On the third day the Sun leaves his wife, the Moon, at his setting place. On the fourth day donkeys begin to see this little wisp of a new Moon and they sing her praises.

It is only on the fifth day that we people can see her. And remember, my child,' instructed Kokoo solemnly, 'never point at that new Moon with your finger. If you do, all the milk will be spilt and there will be nothing for you and your sisters to drink. Only point at the new Moon with your thumb. Put your thumb between your fingers when you point and then the Moon will not mind.'

'Do you know, my child,' asked Kokoo of Nosim during one of these wonderful story sessions, 'why it is that when the Moon dies it always comes to life again and yet when people die that is the end; they never come to life again? It is all because of a dreadful mistake Leeyio made long, long ago.' Now Nosim knew that Leeyio was the father of her people, the first man whom the great Enkai had made, back in the beginning of time, so she settled down next to Kokoo with eyes shining, to hear the story that was coming:

'*Etii apa* ...' started Kokoo in the way that all good stories start, rather like the 'once upon a time' that starts all the stories in English that children like to hear. '*Etii apa* ... there was a great, wise man called Leeyio. He had great sorrow in his heart because of death. He saw how sad people were when a child or a mother or a father died. So one day Enkai, the Great god of the Sky, came and talked to him.

'Son,' said Enkai to Leeyio, 'I have seen your crying over death. I have seen your sorrow over those who die and do not return. Now, if you do as I tell you, then in the future when someone

18

dies, that will not be the end. They will come back to life again. Now listen carefully. The next time a child dies and its body is put outside the village as is the custom, look up to the Moon and say:

'Man, die, and come back again,
 Moon, die, and stay away.'

Soon after the god had told Leeyio this, a child died in the village. It was not Leeyio's own child. There was no great sorrow in Leeyio's own heart. The child was taken out in the evening, outside the great thorn fence surrounding the village, as is the custom when someone dies. Leeyio remembered the god's words and looked up at the Moon shining brightly in the heavens. He thought what a lovely light it gave. He thought how terrible the night would be without its friendly light. So he lifted up his voice and said:

'Man, die, and stay away,
 Moon, die, and come back again.'

When Leeyio returned to the village he heard a wail from his own hut. On entering, he found that his own child, his very own son had died. Desperate with grief, he rushed with the limp body in his hands and laid it tenderly on the ground outside the village. Remembering the words of the god, he looked up at the Moon and cried:

'Man, die, and come back again.
 Moon, die, and stay away.'

But his child remained dead and never returned. Leeyio had spoilt it for all mankind by not following Enkai's words in the first place. Nobody returns from the dead; but each time the Moon dies we know it will come back again.'

And so little Nosim, far off in her first world, started learning the lesson that all the wise of the world must learn: that only sorrow and trouble follow on disobeying the words of the Great Enkai. How different it would all have been, she thought in the silence that followed the story, if only Leeyio had obeyed Enkai the first time.

These stories made Nosim feel wise. She was now able to look up to the great sun and the shining moon and know just why they looked the way they did. She learned too about some of those far-off twinkling stars. Those six stars called the Pleiades were known as six of god's best cattle. They were good stars and the Maasai rejoiced when they could see them. In the months when those shone, the rain was sure to fall and then there was food for all.

In the constellation of Orion, Kokoo saw a funny story of three old widows chasing three old men across the heavens. Nosin could almost see them as she listened to the story. And that bright path called the Milky Way was the road over which the great warriors of the skies were driving their captured cattle back to the manyatta, their village – the halo one sees around the moon some nights.

Kokoo also explained to Nosim why the Maasai were superior to all the other peoples of the earth.

'Etii apa... Leeyio had two sons. When he lay dying he called his two sons to him. First he asked the eldest son what he wanted from his father as an inheritance. Now the elder brother was greedy. He saw this as an opportunity to get much wealth. He asked his father for everything: some cattle, some goats, some donkeys, much land and the food of the ground. Then Leeyio asked his younger son what he wanted. The younger son, so overcome by grief at seeing his father dying, cried out, 'Father, all I want is this fly-whisk in your hand as a remembrance of you.'

Leeyio was pleased with his younger son's love and lack of greed and blessed him and made him the greatest of all people. The greedy elder son got what he wanted; something of everything – a few cows, some scrawny goats and little plots of land. From him descended the prolific agricultural tribes. They labour long in their gardens and by the sweat of their brows produce a little of the food of the earth to feed their children. The Maasai are the descendants of the younger son, the blessed one, the favoured of god; noble folk who do not lower themselves by scratching the earth for food like chickens. To them belong the cattle of the earth – God himself gave them to the Maasai.

Kokoo explained to the eager Nosim about the cattle raids of the brave warrior bands. The government, those strange people who do not understand these things, call it stealing when these great warriors sweep down on a Kikuyu village or a white man's farm and drive off the cattle. But this cannot be called stealing. Did not the great Enkai entrust the cattle of the world into the hands of his favoured ones, the Maasai? The cattle were a gift from Enkai himself. They had come down from the sky, walking down a great strip of rawhide right into the Maasai village. Enkai has so blessed them with cattle that they had had to cry out to their god to stop, for fear of being trampled by this great herd from heaven. So, let the other races – the lesser people, the white men and the Kikuyu – let them till the ground and work for their living by the sweat of their brow. Hoes and labour were not for the Maasai. Nosim's eyes gleamed and her heart swelled with pride. How glad she was that the great Enkai had made her a Maasai!

# Her First World Disturbed

'Today is a very special day!' was the first thought that jumped into Nosim's mind as she woke up one morning. All was still quiet. Kokoo's heavy breathing next to her in the bed was all she could hear. But once Nosim had remembered that this was a very special day she was wide awake and impatient to get up.

'Father is coming home today,' she sang over and over in her mind. Now, all Maasai children love their fathers; and the fathers love their children, and the mothers make very special preparations when father is returning from a journey so that he can be proud of, and pleased with his family. Now that Nosim's arm was no longer painful she was glad it was broken. A special fuss would be made of her when Father heard what had happened. He would call her to him and squat down next to her and ask what had happened. He would look concerned and inspect it to see if it had been straightened well. And when all the rest of the family would be bustling round attending to Father's needs she would be allowed to sit with him and he might even bounce her on his knee as he sat and talked with the elders of the village who would come to hear the news of the villages he had passed through on his journey. Yes, it was going to be a most satisfactory day and she wished heartily that it would begin soon!

Presently, her mother stirred where she lay on the big bed with baby sister. Then she got off the bed with a grunt and Nosim could hear her scratching around in the ashes of last night's fire. She took out a long metal pipe and blew strongly on the still warm coals. Soon a faint red

glow lit up the dark hut. Then Mother reached out to where the firewood was stacked, placed a few sticks on the fire and blew again. Soon a merry fire was burning and Kokoo and big sisters also woke up.

As Mother pushed aside the flimsy wicker-work screen that served as a door, Nosim followed her out into the pale dawn. The cattle were stirring and she could hear the voices of the other women around the village as they chanted their prayers to the morning star. Nosim gazed up at that beautiful star, paling before the coming sun, as her mother lifted up her voice:

'I pray you, who rise yonder, hear me. Keep our cattle safe this day. Bless my children. Take care of our people.'

'Nosim, call your sisters,' said Mother, and Nosim scuttled into the hut to tell her sisters to hurry out to help with the milking. Soon everything was bustle in the village and the day had truly begun.

Nosim took the gourds that had carefully been prepared the day before, to where Mother was starting the milking. Mother began by taking the lid off one of the gourds, milking a little milk from the first cow and then pouring it carefully into the lid. Her sisters paused in their jobs and stood silently as Mother tossed this milk, the first milk of the morning into the air, towards the sun rising in the east, towards the sky, the home of the great Enkai who gives all things.

'God, give us life. God, we beseech you, guard our sons and daughters. God, we ask of You, increase our herds.'

This done, the milking began. Each calf was called – Nosim marvelled how every calf seemed to know its own mother – and while the calf drank from one side, her mother and big sisters milked on the other side, skilfully, straight into

the narrow gourds. In this way calves and people all had their fair share. For of course, to Father, calves were every bit as important as children.

Later Taki and Tombo came over from the boys' hut, glistening and gleaming from the red-ochre and goat-fat they had just smeared liberally on their strong young bodies. Their heads were shaven except for a little tuft right on top. Into this tuft they had each woven a feather and a little string of beads. This now bounced up and down in the approved fashion as they tossed their heads proudly, very conscious of their splendour. They picked up a gourd of milk each and went off by themselves. Men do not take food in the presence of females. A long day was before them and today there would be no slacking or playing. They would tend the cattle diligently, taking them to the very best grass, however far away. But they would take the cattle in the direction they expected Father would come on his way home. Father would be bringing presents – maybe new spears for his boys if he found them working well.

Presently, with many shouts and calls, they set off with the cattle. Other young men went off with their herds. Some of the girls took the calves and goats off to nearer pastures and the morning bustle was over.

But there was still work to be done. Mother's house must be in good repair and so the fresh, still steaming cow-dung was collected up and smeared skilfully on the parts that had cracked and dried in the sun. Then Mother called her daughters to her, one by one. They sat down in front of her and, carefully, she shaved their heads till their scalps were clean and shiny. Carefully she scraped off their eyebrows too. Hair is unbecoming and everyone must look well-groomed for Father's coming. A friend came and shaved Mother's hair too and then they all went inside. Mother took out the big flat skin bag where all their ornaments were kept. They put many of the big bead and wire collars around their necks. They chose out the prettiest earrings to thread through the holes at the tops of their ears. They each put a string of beads round their heads, with the shiny little arrow of tin dangling prettily on their foreheads. Then they smeared themselves liberally, especially their cheeks and necks, with their prized cosmetic – the goat-fat and red-ochre mixture.

At last, dressed in their finery, they went to sit outside – Mother to decorate a new calabash, big sisters to sew beads on to the new leather arm-bands they were making, and Nosim to sit and play with the baby and to rush every few minutes to the gateway in the high thorn fence to see if Father was in sight yet.

Eventually she saw him, with two other men of their village, coming up the slope with the free, springy step that carries these men of the plains for so many miles with ease. Now Mother and big sisters must wait respectfully inside the enclosure and greet him demurely, as befits his dignity. But Nosim was still a child. She rushed down the slope shouting over and over again, 'Eeuo Papa, eeou Papa, Father has come, Father has come,' and was quite breathless by the time she reached the three men.

'Ng'asak,' she said, standing in front of Father and presenting her head for his greeting. Lovingly he placed his hand on her head. 'Child of mine, greetings,' he said. Then she bowed her head to each of the other men in turn and received their greetings. She scampered happily back to Father and confidently put her hand in his as they continued up the hill into the village.

And all the rest of the day was just as satisfactory as she had visualised it in those first glad moments of dawn.

Father made a great fuss over her arm and she was quite the centre of his attention. Others bustled busily about but no one sent her off on an errand or even ordered her off to go and play. She sat next to Father and rested her head on his knee as he sat in the sun hearing the news of the village from the other men and in turn telling them news of the great world outside. Whether she was tired from excitement or sleepy from contentment, who can tell, but she dozed, relaxed and soft as a kitten on the dusty ground. She stirred lazily as Father shifted his position to open his tobacco horn that hung on a chain round his neck.

'I'll tell the Chief she can't go yet because of this broken arm... yes, I did protest but he said I must because our family has not yet sent a child to school...' Just then some other men strode up and Father stood to greet them. Nosim, disturbed from her sleep, got up, stretched and then wandered off with the words she had half heard nagging uneasily at her consciousness. Father had said something about someone with a broken arm. Could he have been talking about her? This someone was to go to school! Could it be she?

Suddenly she felt small and frightened and the sun did not seem to be shining so brightly. She ran off to find Mother and hung around her restlessly as she saw to the preparation of the gourds for the evening's milking. Presently her mother suggested that she clean her own little gourd so that she could fill it with warm

29

sweet milk when the cattle came home at dusk.

Soon she was absorbed in this task. First, she carefully washed it out with a little hot water from the pot on the fire in the hut. Then she put a special stick on the fire, an 'oleirien'. When it was burning well she picked up the end and popped it into the gourd and quickly put her hand over the mouth to stop the smoke getting out.

Then she shook the stick out, put it on the fire and repeated the process over and over again till the inside was sweet and dry and coated with just the right amount of soot from the fragrant smoke that would give a delicious taste to the milk she would put in it that evening.

But in all the familiar activities of the evening, the milking, the chatting round the fire, drinking the delicious 'motori,' or beef-tea, she did not feel again the gayness of the morning. Something disturbing was going to happen. Father was bringing home some news that would affect her. She knew he would not tell them that evening. Bad news is broken only in the morning. But she could not forget those half-heard words which had brought a misty cloud over her happy sun.

As she lay down on the bed that night and snuggled against Kokoo she found little comfort from her bony, leathery body.

# Into a New World

And as she feared, so it happened. While Nosim and her mother were sitting in the smoky hut the next morning, Father came in and sat down. One does not hurry in important business, nor is it the done thing to go straight to the point, so he sat telling Mother the news of his journey.

... No, the Kajiado area had had even less rain than they; the grazing was very poor there ... Yes, he had seen her brother; they were all well in his family, but thinking of moving soon to a greener area... No, he had not walked all the way. He had ridden in the Chief's Land Rover part of the way... he had been glad to see the Chief; he had heard all the news of the great fight between the Purko and the Matapato clans over grazing rights... the Chief was going to the villages of their area to see about children who should go to school that year. Then Father paused and looked solemnly at Nosim:

'The Chief says our family must send a child to school. They say amongst the Council of Elders that our family has not yet sent a child. The Headman suggested that our third daughter is just the right age. Her front teeth have just come out and he says that the white woman

31

at the school for girls likes them to come to school at that age...' He went on talking but Nosim heard no more. She flung herself into her mother's arms and sobbed.

'*Malo, malo*, I won't go!' Mother looked upset and Father was very grave. They disliked very much the idea of sending a child of theirs to school, but they respected the Chief. They knew that other families had had to send a child to school, much as they hated to do it. The government, for some strange reason no Maasai had yet been able to fathom, thought it was a good thing to send children to school. So every year the chiefs had to go around finding out which families had thus far escaped and tell them to send a child. True, some rich men would sometimes give a poorer neighbour a cow or two to persuade him to offer his child instead. But, generally speaking, it was best to bow to the inevitable and send the child off to school – with the sincere hope that he would not be too changed or spoilt by the strange things learnt.

'I'll tell the Chief she has broken an arm. She need not go for another few weeks.' And with that crumb of comfort, he left the hut to rejoin the elders and sit discussing the weightier matters of life; of cattle and grazing and when the next rains could be expected.

Nosim continued to sob rebelliously, so her mother comforted her in the most expedient way.

'All right, all right, little one, I'll tell Father you don't want to go. He won't make you go to school. We'll let you stay at home.' Mother said that just to make her stop crying. It was not really the truth, but why not deceive your child if that would comfort her? Nosim gradually quietened her sobs but that little cloud she had felt coming into her sunny sky the day before had spread further over her sun.

Life went on as before for a few more weeks; but it was not quite the same. All the time Nosim was wondering what that strange other world called school was like. Sometimes part of her was eager to go. She felt important when someone said, 'Oh, is this the little girl who has to go to school?' But at other times she felt terrified. The thought of leaving her mother and travelling in a bus and even seeing white people was enough to frighten the bravest of girls. At last her arm was healed; the bone was straight and strong and the evil day could be put off no longer. It was decided that in four days time, when there would be buses bringing people to the cattle-sale to be held about four hours walk away, Father would take Nosim to school.

Those last days passed with terrifying swiftness. On the final morning at home everyone made such a fuss of her that she was quite glad she had been chosen for school. She felt important with Mother and Kokoo and big sisters crying and even Taki and Tombo hanging round to see her off.

The goodbyes over, she followed Father out the gate and down the slope. Then she looked back. She saw the village getting further and further away. She saw Mother turn round and go back inside – with that she burst into fresh tears and started to rush back. Father grabbed her hand firmly and continued striding on. Running, stumbling beside him, she had no time to look back again and soon they were through the dry river bed, up the next slope and out of sight of the village. After that Father just strode ahead and Nosim did her best to keep up with him. When she lagged behind, the vast loneliness of the plains frightened her and she quickly ran to catch up with him. And when they passed some tall giraffe looking disdainfully down at them from between the feathery acacias she felt safer holding Father's hand.

After walking for what seemed, to a little girl, very many hours they came to the place where the cattle-sale was being held. Father was soon absorbed in the grave business of greeting the Great Ones of the tribe and discussing the virtues of their cattle. Such stock sales held no attraction for her, so Nosim wandered off to where some women and girls were sitting in the shade of a thorn tree. In this tightly knit tribe everyone knows everyone else and soon some of the women recognised her and asked after her village.

'Why are you here? Where is your mother? Where are you going?' came out quite naturally as it is not considered rude at all to ask endless questions.

'My father is taking me to school,' Nosim explained and quickly there were expressions of sympathy and indignation from the group.

'Your father should have refused!' declared one old grandmother.

'When our family was to send a boy last year,' volunteered another woman, 'I carried my youngest son on my back all the way to school. I knew the teacher would say he was too small. He told me to keep him till his front teeth came out and then bring him back. But I told the Chief that I had taken my child and the school had refused him. I did not tell the teacher I had another boy at home just the right size for school. And I did not tell the Chief that I took the wrong boy to school!' Her audience laughed at her smartness and they all felt drawn closer to each other as they discussed other ways in which they could outwit that common and much feared enemy – Change. For anything that might in the slightest degree bring change into their lives, anything which was not exactly as their forefathers had done for generations, was to be fought with all their wiles.

'There is another schoolgirl over there,' spoke up one big girl, pointing in the direction of the bus. There, sitting alone, astride a little wooden box, was a girl just slightly older than Nosim. From the look of her face she was a Maasai, but how different! She had no pretty bead collars, or the familiar ear-rings and she was wearing a strangely shaped cloth of many colours. If that was what a schoolgirl looked like, Nosim was sorrier than ever that she was about to become one. Quickly a friendly woman took

Nosim by the hand and led her over to where this strange-looking girl was sitting.

'Here is a girl who is going to your school,' announced the woman by way of introduction.

'What are you called?' asked the woman, wanting to know her name. 'Who are you of?' she added, asking her father's name.

'I am Titeu of Malit, child of Koisani,' answered the girl. Nosim was horrified. She would never say her name out boldly like that. One did not say one's own name; it was unlucky. These schoolgirls were queer people.

'Well, you tell Nosim all about school. She is going with you on the bus,' said the woman and then she walked off leaving Nosim standing shyly, looking with wonder at this strange girl from school who wore a funny cloth and was not afraid to say her name. But the strange girl smiled nicely at her, moved up on her box and said, 'Come and sit down here. Where is you box?' When she discovered that Nosim had no box she was most concerned.

'You must get a box,' she insisted. 'You need it to keep your dresses in, and also your soap and other things. Have you a dress? It is much nicer to arrive at school in a dress. You don't feel so strange and new.' As Nosim listened to Titeu's prattle all about what one needed in this place called school she got more and more bewildered and frightened. Why had soap and dresses and boxes suddenly become so important? No one in the village had them. School seemed to be a very queer place. Presently Father came over to look for her.

'Papa,' said Nosim, 'this girl, Titeu, is from school and says I must have a box and a dress and a piece of something called soap.'

Father turned and questioned the schoolgirl about it. Importantly she listed the things that schoolgirls think are so essential to life: a dress, knickers, shoes (the highest status symbol), soap and some sweets or chewing gum. This last is the most necessary of all. How else can a new girl make friends? So they all trooped off to the duka – the crowded little general dealer, which sold blankets, maize meal, sugar and other basic essentials of life.

Awkwardly Father announced to the Asian shop-keeper that he wanted to buy a dress for his daughter. He hastened to explain apologetically to the Maasai standing nearby that the Chief was forcing him to send his child to school. He did not want anyone to think that he would buy his daughter a dress and send her

to school of his own free will! They all nodded sympathetically and watched the purchase with interest. Presently the store-keeper came back with a dress he pronounced just the thing for her to wear at school. It was made of the blue and white striped material of which mattresses are made. Nosim took this strange little bag with the three holes and wondered what to do with it. Importantly Titeu took her behind the counter and initiated her into the mysteries of how to put on a dress. It is quite difficult, if you have never tried before, to aim your arms and head for the right holes. Titeu insisted that she must also have another piece of clothing called a 'siruali.' It was another smaller bag with two holes for her legs. That was even harder to put on. Nosim struggled into it but when
she discovered that the bigger bag, called a dress, covered the smaller one, so that you could not even see if someone had one on or not, she decided that this second piece of clothing was quite unnecessary.

Titeu then took off all Nosim's bead collars and ear-rings and wrapped them up in her little red-ochred cloth. Father would take those home. She would not need them at school. Nosim felt desolate at those last reminders of home being taken from her.

Then that stuff called soap was bought. A red piece for her body and a yellow piece for her dress. Nosim wondered what one did with these, but she did not like to ask and the schoolgirl certainly thought they were important. Soap was not used much at home. But school was a place, she had heard, where one learned to do many strange new things. Using soap must be one of them.

But the last purchase Nosim knew and approved of; a handful of those little round sweets that bit the tongue. These and the soap were stowed away in a little wooden suitcase. Father put a small padlock on this. Then he asked the shop-keeper for a piece of string and carefully hung the key round Nosim's neck so that she would not lose it. But he gave the spare key to Titeu to keep round her neck in case she did!

Feeling strange but important, frightened but very excited, Nosim followed Father and her new friend as they climbed into the blue monster called a bus which was to take them to school. Titeu did not seem to be afraid; but Nosim had never been in one of those things before and was thinking it would be nicer to walk.

Suddenly there was an awful roaring noise and the whole bus started shaking. Nosim was terrified and nearly screamed out, but everyone was just sitting calmly as if nothing had happened, so she held on desperately to her seat and tried to be brave. Then suddenly the whole bus lurched forward at an alarming speed and shook even more. Nosim's new-found dignity and over-strained courage left her completely. She let out a shriek and held on to Papa for dear life.

'Take me out of this thing! Let me get off!' she cried. People all round her in the bus had a good laugh and tried to reassure her that no great harm would come to her in this 'blue monster.' But they did not laugh unkindly. They could still remember their first ride in the bus and how frightened they had been.

After a while, when she saw that indeed no harm was coming to her from all the lurching and shaking, she sat up and looked out of the window. How quickly the countryside was rushing by. 'Truly,' she mused, 'if once you get used to the noise and can summon enough courage to stay in the thing, it probably is better than walking.'

But all too soon it was time to get out again. As they came over the brow of a hill, Titeu pointed out a group of big buildings a few miles away.

'That is the girls' school,' she announced importantly. 'We must get off the next time the bus stops.' Now Nosim felt she liked the bus and dreaded getting off.

The bus stopped and Titeu jumped off, eager to greet all the many girls who were coming to meet the bus. They all wore green dresses and there seemed to Nosim to be hundreds of them. While they greeted Titeu noisily, Nosim hung back shyly, but Titeu pointed to her.

'That is a new girl. She comes from near our village. Her name is Nosim,' she announced. The girls crowded around her, stared at her, greeted her, took her by the hand and led her off towards the school. They were only being friendly but there were many of them and she wondered what fresh terror they were leading her to. They told Father they were taking them to see Ng'oto Ntoyie. As Nosim knew, that name meant 'mother of girls' and wondered who her new mother was. Arriving at a doorway, Titeu called out, 'Hodi!' or 'May we come in?' A voice inside said, 'Karibu,' and Father disappeared inside. Nosim followed him quickly, not wanting to be left outside with those girls who stared at her so. She held on to Papa's blanket and peered round to see this Ng'oto Ntoyie.

Just one look was enough and all her courage left her. She let out a shriek, fled out of the house, pushed through the startled bystanders and fled, as fast as her little feet would carry her, back to the bus, the only familiar thing on the horizon, a haven of refuge. She would go back home and nothing would ever make her go to school! That person she had seen in the house, the woman Father was talking to, the one called Ng'oto Ntoyie, was WHITE!

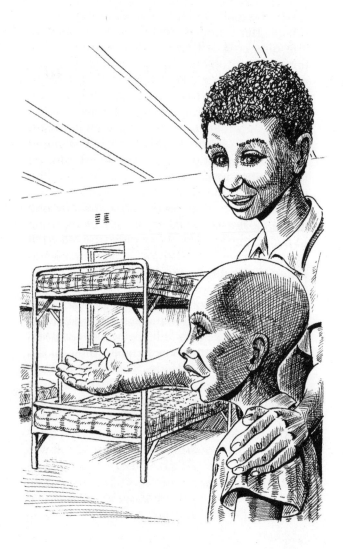

# This Strange New World

Titeu and two other big girls ran after Nosim and caught her. She struggled and screamed as loudly as she could, sure that if she allowed herself to be taken back she would fall into the clutches of that terrifying white woman.

'I also cried when I first saw her,' laughed one of the girls, 'but, really, there is nothing to be afraid of! You soon get used to her white skin and her strange hair. Why, after a few weeks you will even forget that she looks any different.' But Nosim refused to be convinced. She would never get used to anything as strange as that! However, she allowed herself to be led off to a big house they called a dormitory, after they had promised there were no white people there, only Maasai girls like herself.

A big girl called Sintei took her by the hand and led her into one of the rooms in the dormitory.

'You are in my room and that is your bed,' she explained. Nosim looked at the bed. It was not what she thought a bed should be. She was used to a wide dark recess spread with a calfskin which she shared with Granny, big sisters and the baby. How awful to sleep all alone! It would

be cold sleeping by herself on this 'shelf' sort
of thing. Where was the fire to keep them warm
at night? And how could the nice warm air be
kept in with all those big draughty windows?
She sat down on the bed and found it soft and
springy. It was fun to bounce up and down on,
as the other little girls soon taught her – but very
strange to sleep on.

'Ng'oto Ntoyie says I must give you a good
wash and then you must put these on,' said
Sintei, her dormitory 'mother'. Sintei was a big
girl; she had been in school three years already.
She must be very wise after all those years of
school. She handed Nosim some clothes just
like those which all the other girls were wearing.

'Who will lend her some soap?' asked Sintei
of all the girls standing round staring at the
newcomer.

'She has soap,' announced Titeu proudly. 'I
met her at the bus and told her father all the
things she needs for school. She has them in
her box.' Nosim was glad now she had met
Titeu. Everyone seemed impressed because she
had the right things with her. She fumbled for
her key and opened her box. Both the red and
yellow things were soap. She wondered which
one was for washing herself. She picked up the
yellow one.

'Not that one, Silly,' said Titeu. 'That one is
for washing your clothes. The red one is for
washing your body.'

'How much there is to learn in this strange
place called school,' thought Nosim as she

picked up the red soap and her new clothes and followed Sintei and Titeu out to a place they called a bathroom. Sintei had a big, white, soft cloth she called a towel. They went into a little room and took off her two new, little, uncomfortable garments. Titeu reached up and turned a shiny thing on the wall and it started raining – rain inside the house! Nosim let out a scream, both because of fright and the coldness of the water. Titeu turned the little thing on the wall again and it stopped raining.

'What is the matter?' asked the other two laughing, but not unkindly, as they also vividly remembered their first bath!

'That rain – it is cold and makes me wet. Where does it come from?' Titeu and Sintei went off into gales of laughter and explained to her all about the shower, how it worked, and that the water must make her wet so that she could wash and get clean. Then they proceeded with the mysteries of washing. As Nosim understood it that day, washing was like this:

To wash you take off your clothes. You stand in the rain of the little house called the bathroom till you are wet all over. Then you rub yourself all over from head to foot with red soap they called Lifebuoy. Then you stand in the rain again to take all the soap off. Lastly, you rub your body with the big, white, soft cloth called a towel. Doing this leaves big, dark marks on the towel and in the end your body smells funny, like the soap you rub on. Well, that was washing, the first thing Nosim learnt at school, and it seemed a bit silly. She also felt rather bad about smelling so strange. She was used to the accepted smell of the goat-fat Mother rubbed on her skin, but felt a bit ashamed of this new smell of soap, but at least here no one would think any the less of her for it.

After the bath Sintei gave her the school clothes to put on. She was completely mystified. Which one went on first and which way up did it go? But the big girls were enjoying 'mothering' the new girl and helped her into her new school uniform. You put the thing called a blouse on first, Nosim discovered. Sintei fitted the little things called buttons into their holes. That seemed very difficult and Nosim wondered if she would ever be able to do it for herself. Each button had its own hole; you could not just put them into any hole. Then they put the thing they called a tunic on top and tied the belt in a bow at the back. Nosim hoped she would be allowed to keep these clothes on for many days because she would never be able to put them on by herself. When she was all washed and dressed up she felt very strange, but was comforted by the fact that everyone else here smelt and looked just the same. When she was taken back into the dormitory the other girls clapped their hands in delight at the transformation.

Then her father came looking for her. He laughed when he saw her looking so changed and new and pretended not to recognise her.

'School Child,' he teased, 'do not lose your key.' Then he instructed Titeu to take good care of his child and he was gone. Nosim felt desperate to rush out after him; the last familiar bit of home and the old life was going with him. But the other little girls knew how she was feeling because it was not long since they too had been new girls. They bounced her up and down on the bed and gave her sweets and after a few minutes she forgot to be frightened and lonely.

Just then there was a loud noise of two pieces of metal being banged together and all the little girls got up quickly and started running out of the dormitory.

'That is the bell,' explained Sintei. 'It is calling us to the House of Food. Come with me.' Taking her hand, Sintei led Nosim outside to where the girls were getting into a long line outside a big house. They stood in line till the door was opened and then they filed slowly inside and sat down on long benches at tables. On the tables were plates with white stuff the girls called 'ugali,' a stiff porridge made of maize-meal. In a bowl next to the plate were some lovely juicy lumps of meat in fragrant 'motori,' or soup, that Nosim loved so well. Here was something she approved of at school. She was told which bowl was hers so she picked it up and started sipping. Everyone around her looked shocked and Sintei took it from her.

'Wait,' she explained, 'you can't start yet. We must first say thank you to Jesus.' Nosim wondered who Jesus was but when she looked round and saw everyone was waiting, she waited too. After they had all sat down, the woman who was in charge, whom the girls called Mama, made sure that everyone had a plate and bowl and spoon. Then one of the big girls stood up and everyone closed their eyes – everyone, that is, except Nosim. She did not see why she should close her eyes. Someone might take the meat out of her bowl while she was not looking! The big girl who was standing up said thank you, to a person called Jesus, for their food. Nosim looked all around but she could only see Mama and the schoolgirls. She wondered who Jesus was and why they closed their eyes when they thanked Him.

As soon as they opened their eyes again everyone started eating. Nosim picked up her bowl and started drinking the soup. She found there were green things like leaves floating in it and also yellow lumps of something. These she carefully fished out with her fingers and dropped them on the floor. One does not eat leaves and unknown yellow objects. She then chewed away happily on the bits of meat in her bowl.

'Who is this that threw her cabbage and carrots on the floor?' demanded Mama sternly, coming over to the table where Nosim was sitting.

'She is a new girl, Mama,' explained Sintei. 'She only came today.' Mama then greeted Nosim kindly and explained that all that was in her bowl was good food and that she was to eat it.

'Now, eat your ugali,' she instructed. Nosim watched how the other girls did it. They pushed the thing called a spoon into the ugali and when they took it out again there was some ugali on it. This they transported to their mouths on the spoon. It looked quite easy. She tried it, but when she did it, no ugali would come on to the spoon. And when some did, it fell off the spoon long before it reached her mouth. While no one was watching, she picked up some in her fingers and ate. It was quite nice and very quickly filled her up. She wondered how long it took to learn to eat with that thing called a spoon. It seemed difficult.

'Take her to my house, Sintei,' called out Mama as Sintei was leading Nosim out of the House of Food.

Sintei took Nosim to another smaller house and there was something familiar, a fire. They sat down next to it and soon Mama came in and gave them each a mug of lovely thick sour-milk. As Nosim sat sipping it next to the fire, she decided that school was not such a bad place after all.

Again the noise of the two pieces of metal being banged together! 'That's the bell for prayers,' explained Sintei, and Mama told them to run off quickly and get into line.

'The bell seems to rule our lives in this strange place,' thought Nosim as they hurried off. 'Every time the bell speaks it tells us to get into line.' She wondered what this new line-up was for. More food? This time they filed into the big house but there were no plates on the tables and they all sat facing the same direction. A woman called Mwalimu, or teacher, led them in a song that Nosim had never heard, but all the other girls seemed to know it well. It said, 'Jesus loves me.' As Nosim listened, she wondered who this Jesus was. He was the one they had thanked for the food. Then Mwalimu told them a story. It was about a little boy who went on safari and his mother gave him some food to take with him. But instead of eating his food, he gave it to this man Jesus. Jesus divided it out amongst a lot of people, hundreds and hundreds of people. Nosim felt she could not be understanding properly. A little boy could not carry food enough for hundreds and hundreds of people.

'Perhaps,' thought Nosim, 'perhaps it was some of the little boy's food we had for supper this evening. That was why we said thank you to Jesus for it. But why not rather thank the little boy? Oh dear, things are puzzling here at school. They don't seem to fit together like the familiar things of home.'

Nosim noticed that the girls had shut their eyes again. Not all of them though. She noticed that there were quite a lot who were pretending to shut their eyes but were peeping between their fingers and whispering to the girls next to them. The Mwalimu was talking with her eyes shut. Nosim thought she looked very funny, and wondered why she did it.

'... and look after us all tonight, Lord Jesus, and keep us safe till morning,' Mwalimu was praying. This Jesus must be a good person if he gives us food and looks after us all night.

It was a very sleepy Nosim that Sintei led back to the dormitory. 'Take your dress off and get into bed,' she ordered.

'Can't I sleep with it on?' asked Nosim, as she didn't know how to take it off or put it on again the next day. But Sintei insisted and came and helped her. Then Nosim climbed onto the bed and lay down.

'Oh, you Silly, not on top! Open the blankets and get between them.' Nosim opened up her bed and wriggled down inside. So that was how school children kept warm in these strange houses with windows and no fires. It was lovely and soft, warm and cosy.

After the lamp was turned out, Nosim began to feel afraid. She had never slept alone before. Then she remembered that Mwalimu had asked that man, Jesus, to look after them. The song said that Jesus loved them. It was he who had given them their food. Nosim had not seen him but he must be around, somewhere near, because Mwalimu had talked to him.

'I wonder who he is?' thought Nosim sleepily. 'They seem to talk a lot about him here at school. Perhaps I'll see him tomorrow.' And soon the new little schoolgirl, on her first night in the 'New World', was fast asleep.

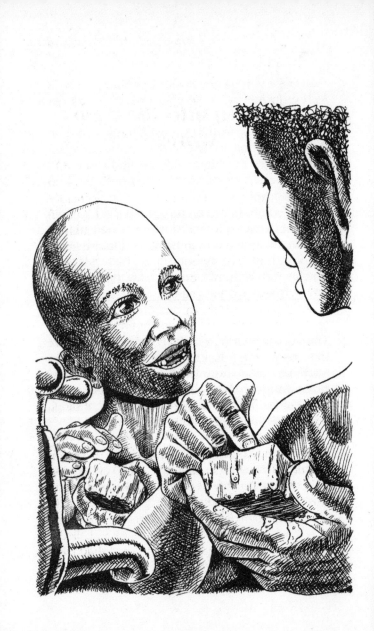

# Settling into the New World

The next morning after drinking some delicious porridge with milk and sugar, and pulling their blankets straight on their beds, and washing again – there seemed to be no end to the times one must wash at school – Sintei took Nosim to a room where there were a lot of other girls, all her size, who were also quite new in school, and left her there with them.

Mwalimu, the teacher came in and told Nosim where to sit. Nosim sat looking around. There were all sorts of funny things to look at. Every time Nosim started talking to the girl next to her, Mwalimu told her to be quiet. It was so hard to remember not to talk. There was so much to talk about. But Mwalimu wanted her to be quiet and listen.

After a while the teacher gave them each a big board to put on the table in front of them. Nosim wondered if they were plates and if they were going to eat again. You never knew what to expect next in this place. Then they were each given a little white stick and Nosim discovered by watching the others that if you rubbed this stick on the thing called a slate, it made nice marks. Soon Nosim had filled up her slate with marks. But the teacher did not seem at all pleased with them and told her to rub them all out again.

'Look at the blackboard carefully, Nosim, and make the marks on your board just like mine.'

Nosim tried. She looked carefully at the blackboard and then made what she thought was just the same mark on her board. True, when she compared them, hers were not exactly like the teacher's. It was much easier to make up her own. But the teacher kept rubbing them out and telling her to try again. Nosim could not see the point of it all but it was nice when her efforts were praised so she tried harder and harder to get them just the same as those on the blackboard. She could not think what these marks on the board were for, but she was very proud when the teacher told the class that the new girl who came yesterday was doing very well and would soon catch them up in writing. So this was writing! The other girls looked at her admiringly. Teacher had praised her on her first day at school. Nosim enjoyed her little moment of triumph. She liked the teacher.

She was quite disappointed when the bell rang and the slates were taken from them. Next they did counting. This seemed much harder. But it was quite fun playing with little stones and bundles of tiny sticks. Some girls counted their fingers, but Mwalimu got cross with them when they did. They must only count the sticks and little stones.

After that they were given books. Nosim looked at them. She had heard of books and had wondered what they were. She opened hers and

looked at the marks inside. Just then Mwalimu
came to her.

'The other way up, Nosim. That is right. Now,
look at this picture. What can you see?' Nosim
looked. Just black lines on white paper. Oh!
The lines seemed to make the shape of a man
standing, a man with a blanket, holding a spear.

'A man,' suggested Nosim timidly. It was so
easy to say and do the wrong thing here at school.
But the teacher was very pleased with her answer.

'Good, Nosim. That is a picture of Papa,
and those marks next to it is the word Papa,
in writing.' And so Nosim read her first word.
After that it was fun. You looked at the picture;
then you guessed what the word next to it was.
There was a picture of an old woman sitting; the
word was Kokoo, and it looked just like Nosim's
grandmother too. But later teacher wrote the
words on the blackboard without the pictures.
Then it was much harder to guess which words
they were.

At last another bell rang and they went out
to play. All this education and sitting for so long
had made her tired. She was very happy when
she saw some swings. They were much higher
and bigger than the swings they made at home
with strips of cow-hide tied to the branch of a
tree. But there were so many girls wanting to
get on whenever someone got off, that Nosim
just had to stand and watch.

Presently the bell rang again and all the girls
ran off. At last Nosim had the swings to herself. She

climbed on to one and was soon swinging up and down, high into the sky and sweeping down again. Yes, the swings at the school were good.

'Nosim, get off there at once and come into class right now!' The teacher sounded angry so Nosim reluctantly dragged her feet to slow herself down and got off sadly. What had she done wrong now? What was wrong with being on the swing? Hadn't all the other girls been swinging just a few minutes before? But Mwalimu took Nosim inside the classroom and she had to listen to a story. All Nosim could think of were those lovely swings outside with no one enjoying them. Later, when she was free to get on them, other girls were there before she got a chance. Why didn't they leave one to enjoy oneself here at school?

Then teacher started teaching them a song. It said, 'God looks after me, God looks after me. Every day, all the time, God looks after me.' Yes, that was something she could understand. Her mother had taught her that at home. Had she not seen her mother toss the first milk of the morning to the sky and ask god to look after them? Yes, Enkai, the great god who made all things, she knew about him. But who was this Jesus they prayed to, here at school?

That evening she saw the white woman again! They were going into the House of Food when Nosim saw that, instead of the Mama who had looked after them the evening before, the white woman was there. She wanted to run away but as soon as she started getting out of line the big girl watching the line pushed her back in place. She watched the girls going inside. No one seemed to be afraid of going quite near the white woman and even talking to her. The girls even smiled when she came near them and spoke to them. So Nosim bravely stayed in line, sat down at her place and started eating her food, all the time hoping that the white woman would not come over to her side of the dining room.

Soon Nosim forgot all about the white woman, and was concentrating on the art of balancing a bit of ugali on her spoon long enough to get it to her mouth. She was becoming more skilful, but still thought it would be much easier to use her fingers.

'Is this Nosim, the new girl?' a voice inquired suddenly behind her. She looked up and there, just behind her, with her hand on her shoulder, was the white woman herself. Nosim felt frightened, but it did reassure her that this strange person spoke her language. True, it did not sound quite right, but you could understand.

'Yes, Ng'oto Ntoyie,' the other little girls around her piped up. 'That is Nosim. She came yesterday. She is the one who ran away.' And they all laughed and seemed to think it was a great joke that anyone should be afraid of the white woman, or Ng'oto Ntoyie, as they all called her. Nosim felt silly. If girls as small as she, were not frightened and could even talk to this strange person, she had better pretend not to be frightened any more either. So she looked up bravely and gave Ng'oto Ntoyie a weak smile and then looked down at her plate very quickly again. She was relieved when Ng'oto Ntoyie went over to the other side of the room and she could once again apply herself to the difficult task of eating with a spoon.

That evening Ng'oto Ntoyie took prayers. Nosim did not feel frightened any more, as long as she did not come too near. She seemed harmless enough and some of the other girls even held her hands as they walked into prayers with her. And her name, Mother of the Girls, she discovered, had been given by the girls themselves. If they called her 'mother' she must be alright. Still, Nosim wished she did not look so strange. But it was while Ng'oto Ntoyie was talking that evening that she found out who that Jesus was, about whom she had been hearing so much at school. He was the Son of God; he was also God, like his Father. Nosim wondered why she had not heard about him before, in her village. In all the stories Kokoo had told her, Jesus, the Son of God, had never been mentioned. Could it be that Father and Mother and Kokoo did not know that God had a Son? Wouldn't the people be interested to hear all she had learnt when she went home for the holidays?

And so the days of her first term at school went by. Every day brought strange, new things to learn. There was a pleasant day called Saturday, when they did not go to classes. The bigger girls had work to do, like scrubbing the dormitory floors and cleaning the windows (although they looked, to Nosim, perfectly clean already). But the little girls, like Nosim, were told to pick up papers that were lying around. That was not very hard work. You just picked up a few papers and walked around with them in your hands and those girls called Prefects, who were supposed to be watching you, thought you were working. Better still, Nosim soon discovered that it was possible to slip off and have a good long time on the swings before anyone discovered you were missing. After that work was over, they just played for the rest of the day. And school had lots of nice new games. Nosim could see much more point to them than to some of the silly things they learned in the classroom. For one of the games, you drew lines on the ground, then you threw a little stone into one of the houses you had drawn, hopped on one leg to your stone and then had to kick it out. The girls liked to play this game with Nosim because she was still new at it and so 'died' very soon by stepping on a line. There was another game she enjoyed, where they all jumped over a big rope being turned by two girls. But Nosim usually had to be one of those turning the rope because she kept catching her foot in the rope. How she looked up to the big girls who had been in school two or three years already and could play hopscotch and skip for a long time without 'dying'. She looked forward to the time when she would attain to such wisdom.

Then there was Sunday. That was even nicer than Saturday. There was no work to do at all, except that you had to wash even cleaner than on other days. Then you just went into a big house called 'Kanisa' with lots of other people, not only

the schoolgirls, and sat and sang and listened to
stories about Jesus. Sometime it went on rather
long, but Nosim did not mind. She just put her
head down on her knees and went to sleep.

Sunday afternoon was the best time of all.
Ng'oto Ntoyie took them for a walk to gather
'ilamuriak' to eat – those delicious black berries
that all Maasai children love picking from the little
thorny bushes that grow near any river bed. Mind
you, there seemed a little confusion as to the real
purpose of the walk. Ng'oto Ntoyie always said she
was taking them to get toothbrushes. Now, the
Maasai clean their teeth every day. They use a little
stick, chewing the end until it looks like a brush
and then cleaning their teeth with that. For some
reason that Nosim could not understand, Ng'oto
Ntoyie did not want them to break sticks off the
trees in the school grounds. She seemed to think
those trees were very important. Sometimes, when
girls were very naughty, they even had to carry tins
of water to put on those trees so that they would
grow. But Nosim could not understand why Ng'oto
Ntoyie wanted them to grow when she did not
use them for firewood or even for toothbrushes.
Nevertheless she was coming to accept that there
were many queer things that white people did that
she would never understand!

So on Sunday afternoon Ng'oto Ntoyie
would call them all and say, 'Let's all go and get
toothbrushes.' And they would all set off on a
lovely walk, collecting berries, eating as many as
they could and filling little tins with some more
to munch in the dormitory later. At the end of
the walk Ng'oto Ntoyie seemed to be upset if you
had no toothbrushes, so, if she was anywhere

near, you picked a few sticks which could serve as toothbrushes during the next week. Yes, Sunday was the best day of all.

Nosim no longer felt strange at school now. She had lots of fun with the other girls. She felt it was a pity they had to spend so much time in the classroom, learning useless things like arithmetic, and sitting listening to the teacher, when there were so many nice things they could be doing. But on the whole she enjoyed the life. She was not at all frightened of Ng'oto Ntoyie any more and even ran up to her when she saw her coming along the path and walked with her, holding her hand. Her pale

face and strange hair did not seem so different any more, now that she was used to them and there were times when you could almost forget that Ng'oto Ntoyie was not a Maasai.

In spite of all this, there were some things that Nosim felt she would never understand about white people. Why did they insist on so much washing? Everyone had to wash in the mornings – every morning – and then again before they went to class in the afternoon. Nosim found too that if she wore a dress for longer than two or three days, Ng'oto Ntoyie said it was dirty and made her wash it. It was true there were some marks on the dress because Nosim had not yet mastered the art of eating with a spoon, but that was food, not dirt. 'Why,' thought Nosim, 'I wear my cloth for weeks at home without washing it.'

The other thing she could not understand was all the hurrying they had to do at school. No sooner had a bell rung than Ng'oto Ntoyie would be outside telling them to hurry. She never seemed to understand how important it was to first finish the game of hop-scotch or whatever they were doing. Wash, wash, hurry, hurry, seemed to be the main things in life for these strange white people.

As it got nearer to holiday time, Nosim became more and more excited. When one of the big girls told her that there were only twelve more days till they went home, Nosim and a friend scratched twelve little marks on their desk and every day they crossed one out. But the last one was never crossed off. That last day they were too excited to do anything in the classrooms. They washed their dresses and scrubbed their boxes and sang goodbye songs until they were worn out. But excitement kept them awake most of the night and they lay whispering excitedly about all they were going to do in the holidays. First on the list of the nice things of home they were anticipating, was all the lovely sour milk they were going to drink.

'Yes,' Nosim decided happily as she shivered with excitement, waiting for the day to dawn, 'quite the nicest part of being at school is going home for the holidays.'

# A Visit to the Old World

Nosim was the first off the bus as it rattled to a stop near the shops where she had first got on it three months before. She could see her mother in a group of women, standing on the verandah of the shop, peering anxiously at the bus.

'Nena nanu! Here I am!' she shouted as she rushed across to her mother, flung her arms around her and buried her face in the old familiar cloth that she loved so well.

'Ai!' exclaimed one of the women in surprise, teasingly. 'Who is this child of the white people?' The women pulled Nosim loose from her mother to have a good look at her. They clapped their hands in mock surprise. They fingered her dress, they pulled the growth of hair on her head and exclaimed over her. But when her mother had kissed her, she just looked up at them and laughed.

'It is me, Nosim,' she stated. 'I am not a child of white people; I am the one who went to school.'

They stopped their teasing and there were greetings from all and Nosim felt that lovely glow in her heart that one gets when one is welcomed; when one is back home amongst one's own people.

Nosim went back to the bus where the driver was unloading goods from the roof, and found her box. Mother took out her skin strap, used for carrying, tied it round Nosim's box and swung it on her back. Soon they were all striding along in single file on the path that led back home. They walked in single file because the path was narrow and called out questions to the excited Nosim. It was wonderful to be so important, to be the centre of attention, to have so much news to tell. She felt so wise and experienced telling these women of faraway places and strange doings!

'What do you learn at this place called school?' they asked. Nosim started explaining, perhaps a little boastfully, of boards on which they made marks with a little white stick, and of the picture of Papa that had marks saying 'papa' next to it. They all thought that was very funny. What could be the use of spending days making marks on a board and looking at pictures? They laughed as they discussed the folly of such useless activities and Nosim felt a little bewildered. At school everyone thought these things very sensible and important. A feeling of being alone, of being different, grew in Nosim's puzzled little heart as the women discussed and laughed at her strange dress, her clean, shining skin and the fact that she had allowed her hair to grow.

But this feeling was quickly forgotten as the last rise was breasted and they could see their home village. Nosim was so excited that she started jumping up and down. She could see the children of her village, her old friends, the ones she had so much news for, come running out of the gateway and stream down the hill towards them.

'Eeuo Nosim!' some of them were shouting. 'Nosim has come!'

But when they actually met they hung back shyly. Nosim felt strange. She had been away to a new world and had come back looking different. Just then her baby sister came toddling down to where they were all standing. This was the little one she had carried around on her back, her special charge, her little sister whom she loved so dearly. She rushed to her to pick her up and love and kiss her. The little one let out a piercing yell and struggled out of her arms. The women laughed.

'See,' they chuckled, 'her own sister does not know her. Truly she has become a white girl, this schoolgirl of ours!' Mother took the baby and they entered the village. She led the way to her own hut. They were home at last. It was good to be back in the old, familiar smoky hut. Everything looked and smelt like home. The thick, cool sour milk was so much nicer than the porridge of school. But Nosim had just a little feeling in her heart that she did not belong in quite the same way as she had before. The smoke stung her eyes and the baby would not come to her.

'Your karash is at the foot of the little bed,' said Mother after Nosim had had a good, long drink of milk. 'Take off your school clothes and put it on, and the baby will not be afraid of you.' She felt in the dark recess she had shared for so long with Granny and her sisters. There she found the bundle Father had taken home three long months ago, when she had put on her dress for the first time, in the shop, behind the counter. She unwrapped it. The cloths were stiff with stale dirt. One she wrapped tightly round her hips, the other she knotted over one shoulder. She put the little bead collar around her neck and the ear-rings through the holes in her ears. Nosim felt guilty. What would Ng'oto Ntoyie or Mwalimu say if they saw her now? But she would not be seeing either of them, or anyone else from school for four long weeks, and she was at home now.

She sat down in front of Mother and had her hair shaved off. At school the girls liked to grow their hair, but at home hair on the head was considered unbecoming. Her mother wet her head with a handful of water and then, carefully, but with rather a blunt blade, she scraped her head until not a hair was left. Now Nosim looked and felt like one of the village again.

By the next day she had forgotten all about feeling different and was playing happily with her old friends. And they wanted to know all about school and what they did there.

'Come and sit over here and let's play school,' she suggested and eagerly her little friends gathered round, bright-eyed, for the fun of a new game. She arranged them in a line in front of her. She tried to be strict, like the teacher was at school and told them to sit up straight and stop talking. They thought that was very funny and talked all the more. She wondered how she was going to teach without slates, but then she remembered how Mwalimu sometimes took them outside and let them practise their writing patterns on the ground. So she told her 'pupils' to clear a little patch in the dust in front of them. She cleared a patch for herself, and, with a little stick, scratched some of the lines and patterns that Mwalimu drew on the blackboard at school.

'You look at those marks,' she instructed. 'Look at them carefully, then you write them on the ground in front of you.'

Her 'pupils' thought this was very funny and looked and scratched with commendable concentration. Nosim acted Mwalimu at her strictest and scolded and rubbed out and told them they were stupid and must try harder. But her pupils did not react in the right way. It was hard playing school with children who had never been to school. They took no notice of her and just made any marks on the ground.

She decided to change to reading class. She made a noise like the bell ringing. Then she scratched 'Kokoo,' 'Papa' and a few other words on the ground.

'Now,' she instructed, 'say these after me.' She pointed to the first word. 'That is Kokoo (grandmother),' she informed them. 'Say "Kokoo".' They said it. She pointed to the next word. 'That is Papa. Say "Papa".' They said it. She pointed to the first word again. 'What is that?' she asked. No one could tell her. They had no idea what they were doing.

71

A Girl of Two Worlds

'Why do you say that is Kokoo?' asked one little boy. 'It doesn't look like Kokoo!'

Nosim went into a long explanation of the book she had in school with the pictures and the word next to them that meant the same.

'I think that you do silly things at school,' stated another little boy, and the others were inclined to agree with him.

Nosim decided to teach them the language of the white people, Kisunku, then surely they would be impressed with her wisdom.

She held up her finger. 'Say after me, "Dees is ah pinka".' With much giggling they said it many times.

'Dat is a put. Dees is ah om. Dat is ah doe. Dees is ah mowt.' They chanted away, pointing at various parts of the body as Nosim instructed. She was a bit uncomfortable about this lesson. Somehow, when she said these words they did not sound like the teacher's English. She was not even sure she was pointing to the right parts of the body. But there was no one there to correct her, and who would know if she was right or wrong? She tried to get her pupils to remember and say these phrases by themselves, but they just laughed. Exasperated, she picked up a little stick and rapped a boy over the knuckles when he did not remember what she had told him. That was part of the game, but how can you play school with children who have never been to school? The little boy took up a stick and hit her back, and soon 'teacher' and 'pupil' were having a fight and Nosim felt she was not doing very well at all.

She decided to give them a drilling lesson. That would be more interesting. 'Stand in a line!' she barked at them, and proceeded to try to hurry them to obedience as Mwalimu did at school – only they did not scuttle into line as school children do when an angry teacher advances! They just stood. She pushed them into place, but they did not stay. She gave up trying to get order and told them to jump. They jumped; but they would not keep time and stopped when they liked. Three of the girls a little older than Nosim decided they had had enough.

'This is a silly game,' they said scornfully. 'Let's go to the river where we were playing yesterday.' They wandered off and Nosim felt her audience was slipping from her. She had thought they would all be so interested in the things she learnt at school. Strange how pointless it all seemed now that she was back at home.

'It is time for a story now,' announced Nosim, desperate to hold on to her few remaining pupils. All children love a story and Nosim knew many new and wonderful ones. Here she felt confident. Eagerly they settled down as she started the story about the blind man who sat beside the road begging, and when he heard that Jesus was passing by, shouted and called to Jesus until Jesus heard him and came over to him and made his eyes better so that he could see.

'Who is Jesus?' asked a little boy at the end of the story.

'Jesus is the Son of Enkai, who lives up in the sky,' she explained.

'Can he make my Granny's eyes better?' asked a small girl.

'He has gone back to heaven,' Nosim explained. 'He is not on earth any more.' But that did not sound right. Ng'oto Ntoyie was always telling them that Jesus was with them to help them and hear their prayers. 'Jesus is still with us,' she explained, 'only we can't see Him now.'

'How do you know he is with you if you can't see him?' said an older boy scornfully. 'Have you ever seen him?'

Nosim admitted she had never seen Him. She felt uncomfortable. No one ever talked like this about Jesus at school. It seemed true when Ng'oto Ntoyie prayed to Jesus to look after them and help them. It did not seem strange there, at school, to pray to someone they could not see. She decided she would have to make it more convincing.

'Oh, Ng'oto Ntoyie has seen him,' she stated, and then added recklessly, 'She has seen him lots of times.' She was determined to convince her sceptical audience, but she felt that things were getting a bit beyond her. She wished Mwalimu or Ng'oto Ntoyie were here to explain it all.

'Let's go and join the others at the river,' suggested someone and soon they were all trooping off. Nosim followed them. She was unhappy. Things had gone wrong. So often at school she had thought of the wonderful times she would have in the holidays impressing the others with her new knowledge. She thought they would all marvel at the wonderful things she had learnt at school – things which seemed so important when the teachers told them.

Here everyone thought they were silly. They even laughed at the stories of Jesus. That hurt her. Everyone at school seemed to love and honour him. It made her uncomfortable to hear someone laughing at and disbelieving what she told them about Jesus.

Down at the river they were having good fun. The children were taking lumps of mud and getting gloriously dirty as they fashioned cattle from the heavy black clay. This was something Nosim loved and she was soon as dirty as everyone else. At first she felt a little guilty about this. Then she remembered that for four long, free weeks no one was going to tell her to wash. No one would mind how dirty she was or how much mud she got on her cloth. She felt free. With reckless abandon she threw herself into the fun and soon had produced some very creditable cattle. Some of her lost prestige was regained when she showed the smaller children how to fashion great curving horns for their cows by putting sticks inside the mud and pushing them deep into the heads so they did not fall off. Truly, the old games did seem more sensible now that she was back home.

Some time later a child came running down to the river. 'Nosim, your father has come and he is calling for you.' She wiped the mud off her hands roughly on the grassy bank and ran up to the village and into her mother's hut where Father was sitting on a low stool near the door. Respectfully she greeted him.

She was very proud when he talked to her as if she were a grown-up and asked her news of the school and her journey and of all her adventures in the big outside world. She felt very important. She knew things that her father did not know.

'Papa,' she ventured after Father had asked all the questions he could think of, 'did you know that Enkai has a Son and his name is Jesus? We learn about him in school. We have heard many stories about him. He is very good and strong.'

Father looked grave. 'Child,' he said, 'Enkai we know; but this Jesus whom you say is God's son, we Maasai know nothing about him. He is the white man's god. Those are just the words of school. We Maasai follow what our fathers told us; what our people have believed since the beginning of our race. Are we 'Iloong'uu,' that we should change our god when white people come and tell us stories about a new god called Jesus?' The 'Iloong'uu' Father referred to, Nosim knew were a neighbouring tribe. The name meant, 'the ones who smell,' because these people had taken to the ways of washing and had the distasteful smell of soap on them!

'Child of mine,' concluded Father gravely, 'you are in school because of the wishes of the Chief, but remember that you are Maasai. You are to follow the ways and beliefs of our people. Now, go off and play and forget all these foolish things you are learning at school.'

When Nosim had left, Father and Mother discussed the problem. 'Our child is getting spoilt by these words of school. She will not grow up a good Maasai woman. We must take her to the Medicine Man for protection against these words.'

And so it was that later in the week Nosim followed her Father as he went to the village of the Medicine Man, leading a great billy-goat as a present for that wise man. A goat was valuable, but it was also important that Nosim be protected against the poison of new ideas that she was exposed to at school. As they made their way home in the evening Nosim had a new charm tied round with a strip of fresh goat skin – skin from the goat they had taken to the Medicine Man in the morning. It would protect her. She would hear new ideas, she would be surrounded by new ways, but she was safe. They would not attract her, would not lure her away; she would remain a true Maasai.

And so, through all the weeks of the holidays, the picture of school faded. When Nosim thought at all of school now, it seemed so silly. What was the point of it all? Always washing, hurrying, standing in line, learning things of no value, obeying the teacher when you wanted to do something else. When the four weeks were over Father asked her, 'Child, is it not time for me to take you back to school? I do not want to get into trouble with the Chief.' But she deceived him and said there were still seven days. At school they had been told that telling lies was bad, but she was not worrying about what they taught at school any more. So she stayed another seven days and then Father took her to the bus. This time she was wearing her dress and she had her box. She travelled on the bus alone and was not at all frightened. And tucked away, out of sight, under her dress, was the charm the Medicine Man had put around her neck. It would protect her against the words of school. They would not so easily mislead her this term. She was not frightened of the white woman any more, but neither was she going to believe all she told her. She knew what school was all about now. She realised that all those words she would hear about Jesus were not for her. She was a Maasai.

# *On Guard in the New World*

'Why are you so late, Nosim?' asked Ng'oto Ntoyie when Nosim went to greet her and report back. 'Why did you not return when the four weeks of holiday were over?'

'I was ill,' declared Nosim defiantly. 'My mother would not let me come back till I was better. Also, my father was not at home to give me money for the bus and there was no one to take me to where I catch the bus,' she added.

'Were you late because of illness or because of the bus money?' persisted Ng'oto Ntoyie. She knew that as more than one reason had been given, probably neither of them was true.

'I was ill and I had no money and I did not know what day school started,' mumbled Nosim, turning her head away and looking at the ground. She felt uncomfortable and fully suspected that Ng'oto Ntoyie was not taking her excuses too gullibly. She felt even more uncomfortable when Ng'oto Ntoyie took her inside her house and gave her some milk to drink. It was not the nice thick sour milk of course, but the warm sweet milk her mother kept for putting in tea.

Nosim went off to the dormitory to put her box down and find her school dress. She discovered that everyone had been moved around in the dormitories and she was not in Sintei's room any more. Nosim was glad of that because Sintei would expect her to be obedient and it was hard not to obey her. She looked for her old friends and soon found that Rakonik was in the same room. She was glad of that. Although Rakonik had been in school a year longer than Nosim, she was still in the first class because she played and did not listen to the teacher. Nosim decided that she would be a good sort of companion.

'When did you come back? Which day did you come to school?' Nosim asked Rakonik.

'Oh, I came back last week,' said Rakonik, 'the day Ng'oto Ntoyie told us to come. We had great fun those first few days of term. We did hardly

any class work, mostly cleaning and cutting
grass and sweeping the paths.'

'Puh!' said Nosim scornfully. 'I had a much
nicer time at home. I would not call work like
cutting grass, fun. I told Ng'oto Ntoyie I was sick.
But I was not sick; I just did not want to come
back so soon. When Father told me to go back
to school, I told him that the days of the holidays
were not yet finished, so I stayed another seven
days. I am going to do that every term. I'm not
coming back to cut grass and work. Puh! Who
wants to cut grass in this silly school?' And so,
before Nosim had even got into the classroom,
the medicine of the Medicine Man was working,
like a tiny drop of poison seeping into her
heart, changing her from a happy little girl into
someone grumbly and cheeky.

When the bell rang, Nosim followed Rakonik
into the classroom. She stood defiantly near the
door, expecting a scolding for being late. But
instead of a scolding, she got a lovely welcome.

'Nosim, I am so glad you are back,' said the
teacher. 'Ng'oto Ntoyie tells me you have been ill. I
hope you are quite better. You must work very hard
in class now because the others learnt new words
in reading last week.' Everyone wanted Nosim to
sit next to her so that she would have the chance
of showing off her knowledge, telling her the new
words they had learnt. Nosim enjoyed the attention.
Little girls like feeling welcome and so her feeling
of defiance soon melted away and she forgot that
she had determined not to learn any more of the
wisdom of school.

Before long she was listening carefully and learning many difficult, new words. They were very difficult because even without pictures you were expected to remember what they said. Later they started their writing lesson. Nosim was glad because always she had been one of the best at writing. Most of the others were given books and pencils, but she was given the old slate and piece of chalk that she had used as a beginner.

'I want a book and pencil too,' demanded Nosim.

'Yes,' said the teacher patiently, 'I would like to give you one. But last week all the others had to get their writing correct for two days before they were given a book. You must do the same.'

Nosim felt cross. Why should she sit with a slate when the others had books? The only other girls who still had slates were the really stupid ones. Was she not one of the best writers in the class? Perhaps because of her anger, perhaps because of the medicine in the little pouch around her neck, who can tell, but her writing that morning was not good. The teacher put some red crosses to mark the parts that were poor and told Nosim to go and write those over again. Nosim was angry. She threw her chalk, the little white stick used for writing, on the floor and refused to do any more.

'Pick up your chalk and go and do your writing, Nosim,' said the teacher firmly.

'I won't!' said Nosim. The words were out before she could think. The class sat up and everyone held her breath. No one had ever

said, 'I won't!' to the teacher before. Mwalimu
looked stern and Nosim felt frightened. Maasai
children do not speak to adults like that. But
then this was at school and Father had said that
school was a silly place. Then she started feeling
important. She had caused quite a stir. Everyone
was looking at her. They probably thought she
was very brave. She felt powerful; she was able
to make the teacher angry.

'Go outside, Nosim,' commanded the teacher.
Nosim got up slowly, grinned at Rakonik and
swaggered out of the classroom. Alone on the
verandah however, with no admiring audience,
she did not feel quite so brave or clever. What
would she say if Ng'oto Ntoyie came by? And
presently Ng'oto Ntoyie did walk by.

'What is the matter, Nosim?' asked the white
woman. 'Why are you out here?'

'I am sick,' mumbled Nosim. 'My head hurts
me.' Usually it was not easy to deceive Ng'oto
Ntoyie in this matter of sickness. There were
many girls at school and it seemed this white
woman had learned the tricks of schoolgirls. But
today she was believing. Or did she just pretend
to believe? She took Nosim to the dispensary
and gave her some medicine for her head. Not
the usual little pills that tasted like oranges,
but the sour ones that were not so pleasant to
take. She told Nosim to go to bed and stay there
all day. She added that it was a pity she was ill
because they were having a special practice for
sports day that afternoon instead of classes. And
all afternoon Nosim lay in bed with a grudge

against the world in general and Ng'oto Ntoyie in particular, while she listened to the excited shouts of the other girls as they practised for the Inter-dormitory Sports.

And so the days went by. Some days she quite forgot about the medicine in the little bag around her neck. She learned many new things and had lots of fun. School was interesting. But on other days she felt that bulge under her uniform and it seemed to remind her to be bad. On those days it was fun to do something that the teacher had said they must not do. It was fun to see her get cross. It made Nosim feel important; not just one of the group; someone who had power. She could disturb the whole class and upset the lesson.

One day Teacher found the medicine in its little pouch around Nosim's neck. They were all standing in line and the teacher was inspecting them to see if they were clean. Nosim did not wash as well as when she first came to school and washing was still a novelty. Mother and Father did not consider it necessary so why should she? And so it happened that, when the teacher was inspecting them, Nosim's shirt was rather dirty. She had turned the collar in so that the black line would not be seen. But the teacher was used to the tricks of schoolgirls and scolded her for wearing such a dirty shirt to school. Then she noticed that there was something tied round Nosim's neck and pulled it up to see it better. When she realised what it was she kept Nosim as the other girls filed into their classrooms.

'Nosim,' she asked kindly, 'what is this you have around your neck?' Nosim hung her head. How could she explain to the teacher?

'It is medicine,' she mumbled at last. 'When I was sick during the holidays my father took me to the Medicine Man. My mother told me I must not take it off.' Very gently, but firmly, the teacher removed the charm.

'Nosim, here at the Mission school we do not believe in the power of the medicine of the witch-doctor. We use medicine from the hospital. We drink it and it helps our sickness. At the Mission we pray to Jesus and He makes us better. You must not trust this sort of thing but rather pray to Jesus.' The teacher tossed the charm into the waste-paper basket as they went into the classroom. Nosim felt frightened without the charm. Father had said she must not take it off. Now she had no defence against the words of school. Father and Mother would be displeased with her when she went home again and the other children would scorn her for having listened to the words of school once more. She sat burning with resentment.

Later, when the teacher went out of the classroom at break time, Nosim crept into the room and fished the precious charm out of the waste-paper basket and went and hid it in her box in the dormitory. She could not wear it any more but perhaps it would still help to have it in her box.

\* \* \*

And so the months went by. Holidays came and she loved the free life of her village. She came back to school and found the discipline and work there more and more irksome. Yet, as the terms went by she, nevertheless, felt increasingly at home in the ways of school. She became accustomed to washing and wearing clothes. Each time she went home on holiday she seemed to fit in less and less to the village ways. She felt uncomfortable if she did not wash.

The little smelly cloth was repulsive. Her friends made new friends and they left her out of their activities. They said that those things were not for schoolgirls. One holiday, when she went home she found that there were only tiny children for her to play with as all the girls of her age had been sent off to the Warriors' village.

Nosim's brother was a Warrior now and she was very proud of him. He had grown his hair long and plaited it into dozens of little ropes and all were bound at the back into a glorious pigtail. She didn't always see him in the holidays as the Warriors lived off in their own big Manyatta. But she did occasionally hear news of their lion hunts and cattle raids. It was an honour to have a Warrior brother. Her mother too was proud to have a Warrior son and always wore the brass coils attached to her ear-straps so that all could see she was the mother of a Warrior.

Whenever Nosim was at school, home seemed so desirable. Whenever she went home she felt out of place. Schoolwork got harder and harder. They learned the tongue of the white people and were supposed to speak it. As she got bigger, Nosim found too that she was expected to do more work. No longer did she just have papers to pick up on Saturdays. Now she had to take her turn at scrubbing floors or tables. She also had to take her turn in sweeping the dormitory in the mornings and no one excused her now if her bed was not made well, as had been the case when she was little.

One fateful day things became unbearable. It was her turn to sweep her end of the dormitory and she could not find a broom. True, she had not looked very well, but it was nearly time for the bell and she had not washed yet. The prefect called her and she said 'I won't!' She would never have said that to Sintei, but this prefect was bossy and she did not like her. Then the bell rang and still she had not washed. She could not go to line dirty so she went and hid behind the shower rooms. When Ng'oto Ntoyie found the dormitory not swept, they looked for her. A girl reported where she was hiding and she was found. She was angry and shamed. The white woman told her to sweep the room and again she said, 'I won't.' As soon as she had said it she was frightened but she pretended to be brave. She picked up the broom and made a show of starting to sweep.

'Come to the office when you have finished, Nosim,' said Ng'oto Ntoyie very gravely. Nosim knew what awaited her in the office. She made up her mind immediately what she would do. She would run away from school. She would go right then, that very morning. She would walk down to the shops where the buses stood and be far away before anyone missed her.

Quickly she took off her school uniform and put on her own little dress. She picked up her box which contained all her belongings. All the girls were in the hall for morning Assembly. She could hear them singing, 'Anywhere with Jesus I can safely go...' No, she was not going with

Jesus. He belonged at school. She was leaving Him behind. She was leaving school and all the strange ways. She was going home to be a real Maasai. She would go off with the other girls to the Warriors' village. She would learn the ways of her people. She crept out of the dormitory and was soon running down the road to the shops. She found the bus which went in the right direction and scrambled onto it.

The man who drove the bus looked at her. 'Are you not a girl of school? It is not the time of holidays. Why are you not in school?' Nosim could not deny that she was a schoolgirl as she had travelled on his bus many times.

'Yes, I am a schoolgirl,' she said sullenly, and in this mood lies came readily to her lips. 'But I have to be sent home. My father has not paid my school fees and I have been told to go and get them.' She felt clever to have thought of such a plausible excuse. Soon the bus started. She looked back and saw the school getting smaller and smaller in the distance. She thought how easy it had been to run away and wondered why she had not done it before. Goodbye to school! Goodbye to reading and writing, to washing and sweeping, to prefects and teachers, to hurrying and obeying. She was free at last.

# Choosing the Old World

As the bus rattled towards her home district Nosim began to feel afraid. What would her father say when she arrived home? He would know it was not holiday time. It was the Chief who had instructed her father to send her to school. What if the Chief heard that she had run away? Would her father get into trouble? Everyone would ask her why she had come home. What could she say? She would have to give a good reason. She must think up one that would make them feel sorry for her; that would win them over to her side so that they would not send her back to school. She could not use the story about school fees that she had told the bus driver. All the village knew that her father had sold a cow at the last cattle-auction and had taken the proceeds to the white woman at the school and paid all the shillings necessary for the whole year at school. No one would think there was any cause for running away. All good mothers beat their daughters when they were naughty, just as all good husbands beat their wives when they were lazy. All Maasai accepted this as part of life. No, it would have to be something more convincing.

Then she had a brainwave. She knew what she would say. She would tell everyone that the food at school was finished and that they had not eaten for five days. The people of her village would understand that. Many times the Maasai had to move because of hunger. They would have no difficulty in believing that.

In a cloud of dust the bus drew up at the shops and Nosim got off slowly. Usually she jumped off eagerly to greet her mother or whoever had come from home to meet her. But this time, of course, there was no one waiting for her. Nobody knew she was coming home. She would have that long walk across the plains by herself.

It was a lonely scene. A few lean chickens pecked at the dust in front of the little shop. The heat haze shimmered on the horizon but nothing else moved. She could hear the far-off tinkle of cow-bells and the shrill rasp of the cicadas in the nearby thorn trees – but not another sound. After the rush of her flight from school, the clatter of the bus and the turmoil and rebellion of her thoughts, the silence was frightening.

She wandered into the little shop but no one was there. Evidently no customers were expected. She coughed and cleared her throat loudly a few times and at last the Indian shop-keeper shuffled out from the back of the shop.

'Will you please keep my box for me?' she requested, explaining where she was going. She promised that the next time someone came from the village it would be fetched. He took her through to a back store where he was unpacking bundles of cotton blankets and stacking them up on the shelves. Nosim made a mental note of these new blankets. It might prove to be information that would please her father. A new consignment of blankets arriving at the local shop was quite an event. To a Maasai man a blanket is not merely a thing to keep one warm at night, but it is his clothing, his overcoat and also his badge of office. The warriors, the women and the children wear cloths; the elders wear blankets. Nosim was glad to have something to tell her father that would please him, as he might be displeased about her running away from school.

The Indian took her box and stowed it away behind some tins of paraffin. Then Nosim used the last two pennies she possessed to buy a handful of the round, white sweets which were in a big bottle on the counter of the shop. She liked the sweets in paper better, but you got more of the round ones for two pennies. She must have something to give her mother and the children when she got home. It was the custom to give gifts when one returned from a journey.

After that there was nothing left but to start out on the path that led home. The sun was high overhead so there were still many hours before it would sink behind the hills ahead of her. The wild animals would be asleep now. It was the best time for travelling, even though it was hot. Later, when the shadows grew longer and it became cooler, the zebra, giraffe, antelope and wildebeest, now all standing motionless, would begin to get restless and scamper away in fright at the slightest rustle in the grass. That was the time the lions and the leopards would be out looking for their evening meal. She thought of the other times she had travelled that path. She had never before been afraid. Usually Father had been there, striding ahead of them, his spear in his hand, or Mother and other women from their village. She had to pass a giraffe which was nibbling the leaves of a thorn tree. But from his great height he did not even deign to notice her and soon she was safely by.

She thought of school and pictured the girls in the classrooms, working hard. She was free of that now. No more silly reading and writing and trying to talk the tongue of the white people. She rejoiced in her freedom. She would be able to do just as she liked for hours every day. No more running for bells and everlasting washing! She felt a little hungry and remembered that her class would be at a

Domestic Science class that afternoon and they were planning to bake cakes. She also remembered that she had missed her lunch. Never mind! She comforted herself with the thought that soon she would be home. There she would have milk in abundance, cold sour, smoky milk, real Maasai food, much nicer than the food they ate at school. But she could not help feeling a little regretful about the cakes her classmates would be eating. Her mother would give her an extra lot of milk to drink when she heard Nosim's story about the schoolgirls not having had food for five days. Yes, that was just the right story to tell!

At last she could see the familiar sight of the little hill near her father's village. She knew that when she reached the top of the next slope she would see her home. It had taken her a long time, but she was nearly home. Then at last she could see it.

Home! But it looked strangely deserted. True, the cattle would be off on the plains or at the salt-lick at this time of the day. But the calves were usually tethered near the village and there should be goats nibbling at the thorn-bushes not far from the gate. Generally, too, some old men were sitting outside, under the shade-tree which took the place of the city-club in the life of the Maasai men. The sounds of the children's voices should reach her if they were playing, as they usually did, in or around the village. The flat roofs of the houses did not look cared for. All Maasai mothers regularly smear fresh cow-dung on the roofs to keep them from cracking and crumbling in the sun. True, it was very dry then, and there was no sign of rain to make them worry about the houses being rainproof, but the rains were hoped for and they should be prepared.

And so, instead of being reassured at the sight of home, a flutter of panic stirred in Nosim's heart. What if the village was deserted? What if all her people had moved? Where would she find them? Where would she sleep that night?

As she reached the gateway she knew it was true. This village was no longer her home. It was merely an empty shell, a deserted site where hyenas skulked and rats scuttled. All the people and their animals had moved away across the plains, somewhere, in search of grazing, in search of an area where the rains had not failed, where grass was still to be found.

They had moved several weeks before, observed the desolate Nosim as she looked at the crumbling structure that had been home

when she was last there. But it was home no
longer. She did not consider sleeping there
or even going inside what had once been her
mother's hut. Young as Nosim was, she knew
what happened to the old folk when these
nomadic people moved. She knew that the aged
men and women who could not manage the trek
across the plains were left, abandoned. This was
not done without heartache and the old were not
unmourned. But life is hard and the trek long
which must be made to save the herds. The old
lie down in their huts and go to sleep. It is better
than dying of exhaustion on the way.

Thus the thought of even glancing into the
hut struck terror into her heart. Her Granny was
old. Dear old Kokoo who told such wonderful
stories. What if they had thought her too old for
the journey? What if Kokoo were there . . .

She turned back and ran along the path
she had travelled so hopefully. She would have
to run all the way if she wanted to get back to
the shop before dark. Even with running, she
doubted if she would make it. Sobbing, tired
and hungry, with only fear keeping her going,
she ran, stumbling and panting, along the
path. The shadows were long and the animals
already becoming restless. She did not dare to
let her mind think of anything but getting back
to the safety of the shop. Why, oh why had she
left school? It was supper time there now. She
would be sitting down to a steaming bowl of
stew if she were still at school. Later, the other
girls would be gathered in the lamplight, safe,

behind closed doors, singing and listening to a story about Jesus.

'Kirripito Jesu' – Jesus cares for you – the words of the song they had sung so often came to her mind, but they brought no comfort. Maybe Jesus looked after them at school. Certainly, the teachers seemed to think so. But she had run away from school. She had run away from Jesus. She had turned her back on all those things she had learned at school. How she wished she could cry to Him now and ask Him to look after her – she was very frightened. Somehow she managed to continue stumbling along the path even after it was completely dark. The only crumb of comfort was the far-off, twinkling light she could see in the window of the shop. Gradually it got nearer, and then at last she had arrived.

She banged on the door. 'Hodi, please let me in!' she called urgently.

'It's me. The owner of the box. The girl who came on the bus.'

When the bolt was slipped and the door opened just a crack, Nosim pushed her way in, glad of light and company at last. The Indian was very sympathetic when she told him the story. He scolded her for being out at night and proceeded to warn her of all the terrible things that might have happened to her.

Soon she was sitting beside the fire in the little kitchen at the back of the shop, sipping tea with the shop-keeper's wife. It was not very pleasant tea. It was scented and spiced the way the Indians like it, but Nosim was beyond being fussy. It was hot and sweet and milky and it comforted her. The Indian woman spoke only her own language, but after her husband had explained to her what had happened to Nosim, she smiled kindly at her and looked concerned and motherly. Quite soon Nosim felt safe and relaxed. Not long afterwards she was curled up on a sack behind the counter with one of the new blankets from the shelves thrown over her. After the horror of the ghost village and the terror of her journey in the dark, she felt safe and secure. Tomorrow everything would come right. She would discover where her family had moved to and she would find them. Almost immediately she was asleep.

# Back in the Old World

She did find her family the next day. The kindly
Indian questioned his customers and as everyone
knows everyone else in Maasailand, he soon
found someone who could tell her just where to
find them. The motherly woman gave her some
food – the kind that Indians eat, that burns the
throat and makes the eyes water. They gave her a
shilling and put her on the bus, telling the driver
exactly where to put her off.

When they arrived, the driver took her into
the shop beside the road. Nosim had never
been there before but every little trading post
was the same. A small corrugated iron outpost
of civilisation, with chickens and goats and dust,
a few customers sleeping on the verandah and
a few more chatting at the counter. The wares
are the same everywhere. The main stock is
blankets, cloth and beads. Tins of paraffin and
sacks of sugar form convenient seats for the
customers who are never in a hurry. Purchases
are made at a leisurely pace and every item
must be bargained over: tea-leaves to boil,
tobacco to chew, a few more strings of beads for
making their attractive ornaments, and perhaps
some chips of rock soda to chew along with the
tobacco. And always a few sweets are begged

for and the patient Indian dips his hand into the big bottle on the counter.

To her delight Nosim saw a woman from their village. Quickly she went to greet her and was soon hearing all the news; when they had moved, where they had built their new dwellings, and how everyone was. Nosim told her story too – of the five days of hunger when the food at school ran out, of the journey home and of finding the deserted village.

Presently, when the woman's purchases were all made and Nosim's story had been told to the sympathetic bystanders, they linked up with two men who were driving some goats home and together they set off for the new village.

Her arrival was a great surprise and very quickly everyone gathered round to hear her news. There was a lot of indignant wagging of heads as she told how hungry the schoolgirls were. The sympathies of the women were all with Nosim and they were quick to believe that school was a bad place and that the white woman was starving their children. They had always been suspicious of that place called school so now they had an abundance of 'I-told-you-so' remarks to pass. Nosim also told of her visit to the empty village the day before. As she recounted these stories over and over to each fresh audience, the first seemed to become to her just as true as the second. The imagined hunger and ill-treatment became as real to her as the horror and loneliness of the deserted village.

Soon Nosim was in her mother's new hut, drinking the cold sour-milk she had longed for the previous day. The hut was new, yet it felt like home. Built on exactly the same pattern as the old one, it was already well smoked, with sooty cobwebs hanging from the beams overhead.

But one thing was missing - Kokoo. Her old grandmother was nowhere to be seen. It just did not seem like home without her old Granny who had sat and told her tales of long ago. She was not in the shade at the side of the house, nor yet in the dark recess of the small-bed where the old woman slept. When Nosim asked her big sister where her Granny was she just turned her head and talked of other things. Then Nosim knew that Kokoo was dead. In the Maasai one does not talk of the dead. They have ceased to exist. But Nosim felt frightened when she thought of Kokoo. Where was she, really, now? At school everyone was sure that death was not the end. Had Kokoo gone to God's village or had she gone to that other place - a lake of fire or something like that? At school they were taught that one could only go to God's village if one believed in the Lord Jesus. He was the way there. He was the gateway in. Perhaps she should have told Kokoo about Jesus who was the gate to God's village. Then Nosim tried to remind herself that she had left school and no longer had to believe those things.

And so Nosim's home-coming was not as happy as she had imagined it would be. She was glad Father was away. She hoped he would believe her story, but she was relieved she could delay telling it to him for a while.

For her former play-mates who asked questions about the far-off world of school, she now had very emphatic answers. School was a bad place. You were starved at school. School was pointless. The things they taught were meaningless. Who cared what marks on paper said? What had all that to do with life, which was to them the routine of a Maasai cattle village? School was a prison. They constantly told one at school, 'Do this, don't do that!' School might be all very well for the other tribes whose life was one of drudgery anyway - but not for the free, proud Maasai.

One day a little boy, listening to all this, turned to Nosim with a puzzled look.

'What about Jesus, God's Son, about whom you used to tell us? You said he loved us and came to save us from our sins. Isn't he at your school any longer?'

'Oh, you silly!' exploded Nosim. 'He was not really at my school. They only said he was. We never saw him. Probably all they told us about him was just foolish talk, like all the other things they told us at school. They just made that up. It was not really true!'

The little boy turned away with tears of disappointment in his eyes and ran off. Nosim felt uncomfortable. She felt very sad too; bad and sort of empty. She tried to shake off the feeling by making up even wilder stories of how the girls had been ill-treated, of senseless lessons and unreasonable discipline. But that night and for many nights afterwards she could not forget the look of disappointment on the little boy's face or the strange, sad emptiness that had settled in her heart when she had poured scorn on her earlier love for the Jesus of her school.

Nosim also found that life was not quite as free as she had thought it would be. She was no longer a tiny child and there was work to be done. Usually, in the holidays, she was petted and spoiled. She was only home for a few weeks so they let her off most of the hard jobs. Now she was not regarded as a schoolgirl any more. She must pull her weight in the tasks around the village. She had long, hot days out on the plains, taking the cattle to water. To her annoyance she found that girls younger than she could carry those heavy four-gallon water tins full to the brim. To Nosim they were very heavy. She tried not filling the tin right up, thinking that would make it lighter. But it was even more difficult to carry because the water sloshed from side to side in the tin, nearly throwing her off balance. She tried to hide the fact that the best she could manage was a small tin. The other girls laughed at her when they saw the miserable bundle of twigs she collected when they went out for fire-wood. She soon learned to cut thicker pieces and stagger home under bigger loads. She had to rise before dawn to help with the milking. Occasionally she thought enviously of the schoolgirls who would still be snuggling under their blankets. Although she loved the milk she drank each day, she often felt hungry, having got used to the three regular meals a day at school. At home there was no regular time to eat. You just drank some milk when you felt hungry. Two or three great mugs of milk after the morning work was done, satisfied her for a while, but she longed for some meat. At school they had meat every day - just a little in the evening stew. At home meat was only eaten on special occasions, when an ox was slaughtered. But then it was better than at school. The meat wasn't boiled, but roasted lightly over the fire so that it was juicy and could be chewed for a long, long time. You ate all you could and of course you had no milk that day. Taking meat and milk together, on the same day, just wasn't done. You didn't even mind the day of fasting after a meat-feast - it was good just to lie in the sun like a lion after a kill.

One day her father came home and listened gravely to her story. He was indignant. Had he not paid 50 rupia (two shilling pieces) to the white woman? What did the school do with all that money? Why were they starving the girls and sending them home? To Nosim's dismay Father said that he was going straight off to see the Chief and demand that he get his money back from the school. She argued hopefully with Father that as school was a silly place, and as she was home now, they might as well just leave the matter. Father calmed down after a while but vowed that the next time he saw the Chief he would tell him all about it. Nosim hoped fervently that it would be a long time before father saw the Chief, and that he would forget the matter; but her hopes were not realised.

A few days later a Land Rover rattled up to the village and the Chief and a few of the elders of the tribe got out. The elders of the village received them with great dignity and formality and soon all the men were sitting under the shade-tree discussing the weighty matters of their people while the women and children withdrew respectfully inside the enclosure.

After many other matters had been discussed, the Chief turned to Nosim's father.

'The white woman from the Girls' School has informed me about your daughter. She says your child has run away from school.'

'She was sent away, O Chief. She did not run away. The food at school was finished and she was told to go home. She was very hungry when she arrived home. She said she had not eaten for five days.'

Father's shame and indignation knew no bounds when the Chief and the other elders assured him that her story could not be true. Had they not been at the school themselves two days before? Were the other girls not still at school and obviously not starving? Had the men not walked round the school and chatted to the girls from their home districts and all was well? Had Ng'oto Ntoyie not told them herself that Nosim had run away one morning because she did not want to do the work of sweeping the dormitory? At last the chief and elders got up to go.

'I will take her back myself and hear the truth of the words from the people at school,' promised Nosim's father. A very frightened Nosim waited in the village as she saw the Land Rover take off in a cloud of dust.

Father beckoned to a child.

'Go and call my second youngest daughter for me. That schoolgirl...' he added, with a note of disgust in his voice.

'Why did you run away from school?' he asked sternly when Nosim approached reluctantly, yet afraid to disobey.

'I was hungry,' she mumbled sullenly. Then her father told her what the Chief had said and she hung her head and remained silent.

With cold, scornful anger he took her by the arm and strode towards the nearest thornbush. Deliberately he took off a long branch. Then he began to beat her – not the feeble slap of exasperation that the teacher sometimes gave the children at school; not the tooth-and-nail sort of beating that she occasionally got when she quarrelled with a girl over some petty matter in the dormitory. This was the real thing. Father had been shamed before the great ones of the

Tribe. He had been taken in by a girl's story. He was to have all the bother of taking her back to school. Truly, this school business caused a lot of unnecessary trouble. He put all his indignation and hurt pride into the blows that rained down on Nosim. The thorns raked her arms and back as she cowered before him, covering her face with her hands.

'*Tapalakaki*!' she cried, 'Forgive me! I'll never do it again. *Maitoki*!'

'These schoolgirls are soft and cry easily,' was the thought that crossed Father's mind as, in disgust, he threw down the stick and strode off. Nosim, bleeding and sore, crept into her mother's hut and crawled onto the bed where she hid herself in the dark recess and sobbed herself to sleep.

She was in disgrace for the remaining few days at home, till Father announced that there would be a bus going the next day, at the place where the cattle sale was held, so they would set off early in the morning.

She left without the treasured tin of butter-fat that every school-child loves to take back to school to eat. Her mother dared not show her any mark of favour when she was under Father's displeasure. As it was, her husband's other wives had been taking advantage of Nosim's lack of favour to taunt her. Not that anyone thought that telling a lie was a bad thing. Everyone tells lies when it is the convenient thing to do. But Father had been inconvenienced and shamed – that was a crime indeed! Nosim could not ask Father for any money so she would not even have a few pennies for *inkitumbuani* –those sodden, doughy fried cakes that all school children delight in buying at the shops at any and every opportunity. She would have nothing to give the other girls in the dormitory. Nothing – just when she so much needed something to boost her morale. Back at school, shamed before everyone, her pride hurt – she would have to put on a very 'don't care' attitude to hide her shame.

Arriving back at school was not as bad as she had expected. She was welcomed back eagerly by her friends, but there was an air of suppressed excitement as they saw Father stride into Ng'oto Ntoyie's office.

'Why are you not giving my child any food to eat?' he demanded. 'I have paid all the shillings for her school fees. Why are you starving her?' Patiently the white woman explained to the man that there was no truth in Nosim's story. He was quickly convinced because he no longer believed it himself. After a while the frightened Nosim was called in and scolded afresh. Her father commanded her to obey the white woman and stay in school so as not to waste the shillings he had paid. He strode out without a goodbye and Nosim was left alone with Ng'oto Ntoyie.

'We have been praying that you would come back, Nosim,' said the white woman. 'We have prayed that every day since you ran away.' That surprised Nosim. She knew she was a nuisance and quite naughty. Why did they want her back?

'You have been with us for a long time already,' went on Ng'oto Ntoyie, 'but you have not yet let Jesus change your heart. We are so glad you have been brought back. Now you will have another chance to hear God's Word.' Nosim's defiant attitude and rebellious thoughts melted a little at the loving words. But she was glad when the supper bell rang and she could run off and join the others in line.

That evening in prayers the teacher told them about the younger son who ran away from home and was received back by his father and given such a loving welcome. Nosim felt uncomfortable. It sounded a bit like her, except she had not come back because she was sorry. She had been brought back. Perhaps that was why Ng'oto Ntoyie had said she should have her heart changed. She should feel sorry. She should come and say, 'Father, I have sinned,' like the younger son. But she did not feel sorry. Her young Maasai heart was proud and did not readily say sorry.

# An Even Newer World

All the excitement of running away and being brought back to school was soon forgotten in the great excitement of a new adventure. And to think she might have missed it if she had stayed at home!

Nosim, and all the girls of her class were to go to Nairobi to see the wonders of the Agricultural Show. She had no idea what the Show was, but she knew that every year the girls of the fourth class set off, early one morning, in a bus, to go to Nairobi, and came back that night with wonderful tales of strange places and incredible things. Each year it was the talk of the school for days beforehand and for weeks afterwards. And now it was her turn to go.

The first task in preparation for the great day was to go around borrowing. Nosim found she was at a disadvantage as some of the other girls had already borrowed the best things. Also, she had no sweets and chewing-gum or tins of butter-fat. These things are essential for bartering or borrowing an especially attractive jersey or head-cloth. But everyone was quite willing, in fact, eager to lend their things to the girls going to the Show. It gave them a feeling of joining in with the Great Adventure. Soon

Nosim was suitably equipped with jersey, head-cloth, handkerchief and shoes. The last was an especially important item, shoes being a highly prized status symbol. Some girls even thought it necessary to go around borrowing pretty underwear for the occasion. No one, it is true, would know if your slip had lace on it or not, but it was grand to go to Nairobi decked out in everyone's finery and feel the well-dressed-lady for the great day.

During the week before the Show, the Standard Four class tried extra hard to be good. But in actual fact they made more noise than in all the other weeks of term put together. For one awful hour Nosim thought she would not be allowed to go. The bus was not big enough for everyone, so some would have to stay behind. Only the ones who had been obedient and helpful enough would go, the teacher explained, with a meaning look at Nosim. But then came the joyous news that Ng'oto Ntoyie would take her car too; then everyone could go.

At last the great day arrived. They were up before dawn, running around getting ready a full hour before they needed to, but, of course, when the bus was ready to go several were still racing around, frantically looking for lost head-cloths and borrowed shoes. The rest of the school waved the bus off and Nosim and her friends settled down in their seats to sing and shout for the whole two hours' ride into the City.

But they saw the first wonders long before they reached the show-grounds. A double-decker bus caused great excitement. Were people not afraid to go in it? Would it not tip over? Who drove the top half? No one! But if there was no driver up there, how did the top half stay with the lower half so well?

And the buildings of the city! They were beyond belief. Surely their eyes were deceiving them! How did people get up to the top?

But the greatest wonder of all to these girls from the lonely nomadic life on the vast plains of southern Kenya was the multitude of people. People and motor-cars wherever one looked! Hundreds upon hundreds of cars and thousands upon thousands of people – all busy – all rushing around. They all looked as though they had somewhere to go and something to do. And no one seemed afraid of crossing the street. With all those rushing motor-cars, the girls had quickly made up their minds that if they ever had to come to Nairobi, one thing they would never do was cross the street – that was surely more dangerous than facing any lion or leopard out on the plains. Truly, this world is bigger and there were more people in it than they had ever thought possible!

As for the wonders of the Show, they were past telling. Eager eyes and ears were drinking in all sorts of marvels, storing them up for that time, back at school, when they would have an admiring audience, interested in every detail. However, many of the exhibits were beyond their experience and they looked with uncomprehending eyes. But others were well within their grasp. Why! There were cows such as no Maasai had ever seen; cows that could give eight gallons of milk in one day. Two paraffin tins full! Enough to feed a whole village and to spare. The stunted, hardy Maasai cattle give about a cupful a day, and that grudgingly!

And those creatures over there? No, they couldn't be sheep. They were nothing like the sheep at home which just have short, brown hair. These magnificent animals had wool as deep as their fingers were long! Truly, these animals of the white people were things of wonder.

But some girls did not always understand what it was they were supposed to be seeing. One group went into a stand where gas-cookers were being demonstrated. The teacher expected the girls to be filled with wonder at seeing fire burning with no wood. They scarcely noticed that. What caught their attention and filled them with amazement was the green eye-shadow worn by the lady demonstrator. (This wonder of wonders was shared at school the next day, with the help of green black-board chalk!)

The trip home in the evening was quite as exciting as the ride in the morning. There was so much to talk about. The arrival back at school was by no means an anti-climax. In fact it proved to be the best part of the day. Each returning hero was soon the centre of an excited group of listeners; and stories lost nothing as they were told and retold far into the night.

Another day of wonder, one that Nosim would never forget, was that triumphant day when the choir, a group of little starry-eyed Maasai girls, came first in their section in the Kenya Music Festival.

The song was difficult, but as they practised, the girls felt sure they would win. The teacher was not so confident. She knew how raw these little girls were, but it would be good experience for them to hear the other competing choirs and they would learn from it. But it never entered the heads of those little Maasai girls that anyone might be able to sing better than they.

Their confidence ebbed a little as they saw the sophisticated city choirs. But these opponents of theirs – who were they? Were they not white children, Indians, Kikuyu? Was not the reputation of the Maasai people at stake? Had a Kikuyu ever defeated a Maasai in straight battle? So they sang as they had never sung before. Perhaps it was the joyous confidence in their voices, but the only one in the whole auditorium who was surprised when they were announced as the winners was their teacher! But she was so surprised and happy about it that she managed to get a telephone message back to the school several hours before the triumphant choir was due home. What excitement! Every car or lorry that appeared on the road might be the choir returning, so scores of girls would rush out to the road to cheer it on its way.

When the lorry carrying the choir did eventually appear, their jubilation knew no bounds. No Caesar entering Rome in Triumphal Procession ever had greater welcome. Three hundred excited girls rushed out and escorted the lorry the last couple of hundred yards back to the school.

'We have won! We came first!' chanted the girls in jubilation – even those who had never sung a note, but were sharing in the glory of their school's victory. They had always thought that the Maasai were the best – now they had proved it.

These, and many excitements and wonders helped Nosim to settle down to school. True, there was work and plenty of it, but it was interesting. Lessons were getting harder and harder as she got older, but she was seeing and hearing of things that she had never dreamed of in her village and she was content to stay. She was changed too in many ways; in her interests and her outlook. But often she thought of Ng'oto Ntoyie's words to her the day she had been brought back to school by her father... 'We have prayed for you every day. You have not yet let Jesus change your heart...' and she felt uncomfortable. Nosim knew that although school was changing her life in outward things, she had not yet allowed Jesus, about whom she had heard so much, come into her heart and change her inwardly.

# The Pull of Two Worlds

However settled she felt in school while she was there, the holiday times always unsettled Nosim again.

Once, when she went home for the school holidays she found the village in a state of great excitement. Preparations were being made for the initiation rites of her great friend, Lilapa. Nosim and Lilapa had played together as children. They had gone for wood and water together as they got older. Lilapa was scornful of Nosim's ways but the bond was still strong between them. Now Lilapa was going to be prepared for marriage. She would soon be leaving the ranks of the girls to become a woman.

There was much activity in the village. The women who were friends and relatives of Lilapa's mother were busy brewing beer. There must be enough for all who might come to the ceremony. Gourds were being smoked and milk being stored away. Many people would come to sing and celebrate with them and there must be enough food to feed them all well.

The great day came. Lilapa was prepared and left alone in her mother's hut. A hole was made in the roof, near the entrance where she lay so that Enkai, the Great One in the sky, might look down in blessing on her – and also so that the old woman might see to perform the ceremony. The old woman went into the hut and all was still... she came out – it was all over and everyone could rejoice. Lilapa had not cried out so the celebrations could go ahead with no shadow on them. For, the woman whose daughter cried out in pain was ashamed - but not as ashamed as if her son had cried out. That was disgrace indeed! She would go off and hide for fear of a beating, and for the shame of having brought a coward into the world.

Now Lilapa's friends, dressed in their finery, sang and danced outside the hut. The women joined them and sang and danced till they were tired. Suddenly all the children rushed to the gate in great excitement. A procession of women and girls from a neighbouring village were forming at the entrance. They got into a double line, as was the fashion, and advanced slowly through the gate, round the village and stopped outside the house of the woman whose daughter was being honoured. By the time they were getting tired and had finished singing the praises of the girl and her mother, another group was forming at the gate. So it went on all day and far into the night, only to start again with renewed vigour the next day. Nosim, quite forgetting she was a schoolgirl, abandoned herself to the feasting and dancing and singing. Her body tingled and the blood thumped as it coursed through her veins. Truly, nothing in school-life offered any excitement like this.

After all the feasting was over, life seemed dull. Nosim felt cheated. She would like a fuss made of her, like it had been of her friend, Lilapa. Were they not the same age? Should she not also be prepared for marriage? She knew her teachers said it was better to stay in school a few years longer – but all the girls Nosim knew in the villages were married by the time they were thirteen. So when her mother talked about her initiation she agreed and it was decided that the next time she came home for the holidays everything would be in readiness and she too would be initiated; she too would become a real Maasai woman.

Back at school she occasionally felt stabs of conscience as she remembered this arrangement. Everyone considered her a Christian.

Each week she attended the class run by the Pastor to prepare people for baptism. She was supposed to have turned her back on the old ways of the tribe. She followed the new ways in her head and the old ways in her heart. At home they were preparing for her tribal initiation which the Pastor at school told her was bad. At school she was being prepared for Christian initiation which the people at home would despise. She felt very uncomfortable. Outwardly she was different, but inside she was still the same.

'Perhaps being baptised will make me different inside,' thought Nosim hopefully. 'When I go into the water the old ways will be washed away and I will become a new person.'

At last the day came when the candidates for baptism were called before the elders of the church to be examined. She knew all the answers. She could rattle them off pat. Even the all-important one: Do you believe in Jesus? 'Yes,' she could say confidently, 'I believe in Jesus. I believe He came to die for my sins. I believe that He gives eternal life to those who believe.' Of course she believed. She did not think that Ng'oto Ntoyie had deceived her, or that the Pastor was preaching lies. But poor Nosim

did not even know that she was just believing the truth of the words, not believing on Jesus. She did not even know there was far more to Christianity than she had received. That would only come when she let the belief get past her head and into her heart.

To her the all-important part was the choice of a name. She, and the others who had only tribal names, could choose their own Christian names. The Pastor suggested it should be from the Bible so they sat with the Scriptures, paging through, looking for interesting names. It took all Ng'oto Ntoyie's skill to guide them past undesirable names like Jezebel and unusual ones like Kerenhappuch, but in the end Nosim chose the name of Ruth. And Ng'oto Ntoyie prayed that, like Ruth of old, Nosim would choose to stay with the people of God.

On the day of her baptism Nosim was quite nervous. The candidates lined up at the front of the church and one by one they went forward. When her turn came, Nosim, the Maasai girl, went down into the water, and Ruth, the Christian came out – or so she understood it. But deep in her heart she knew she was still the same girl, just with a different name. Again she remembered the words of Ng'oto Ntoyie to her when she was still a little girl: 'You have not yet let Jesus change your heart.' Often, as she sat in church or in evening prayers, she had heard of the peace and the joy and the victory over sin that Jesus brought, and she knew she had none of these.

Now that Nosim was, as she thought, a Christian she had to act like one. She took her turn in leading in prayer at meetings – and secretly thought that she did better than some of the other, more experienced ones! She offered to teach the little ones in the Sunday School and found it more satisfying than her attempts at telling the stories to the children in her village so many years before.

The holidays were coming nearer and she remembered the arrangement that had been made the last time she was at home. She knew that if she went back to her village she would be expected to go through the tribal initiation rites. She thought of all the beer drinking and the dancing. She thought of the initiation ceremony and knew that the Pastor had taught them it was wrong. She sighed as she remembered how much she had enjoyed Lilapa's ceremony the previous holidays. But that was before she had been baptised. She was a Christian now. She should not want these things any more. She did, but she was ashamed to admit it.

Just a week before the holidays were to begin, Titeu, who was now her classmate, told her that she had decided to stay at school for the holidays. She had had a message from her village that her father was planning to keep her out of school and have her ears pierced, which they all knew was the first step to being initiated and married. Nosim decided to stay too. They went to Ng'oto Ntoyie and told her their story. She was very happy. Here were two

Christian girls who had broken with the old ways; who were willing to stay at school during the holiday time rather than submit to traditional practices.

So, when the other girls went off home, Nosim and Titeu stayed. School was very quiet and lonely, but there were compensations. One day they went to Nairobi with Ng'oto Ntoyie and had a wonderful time. They visited the Nairobi Airport and saw huge jet aeroplanes arriving from overseas. Who would have thought that those tiny things one sees high up in the sky were in reality so big, made such a noise and carried so many people! They had a meal with Ng'oto Ntoyie in a restaurant. What strange food Europeans eat! Little bits of different kinds of food all on one plate. But even stranger were the things they used to eat with! Instead of the comfortable spoon, which Nosim could long since use with skill, they held a knife in one hand, and in the left hand, a funny thing called a fork. It had four points with spaces in between for the food to fall through. One was supposed to use it upside down too! Nosim and Titeu took a long time chasing these little bits of food round and round the plate and then gave up. Nairobi was a place of wonders, but it was a relief to be back at school and to have some of the thick ugali they made for themselves from maize flour. Day by day they played and slept and cooked and did not very often think of home.

Then one day her mother arrived. A wave of homesickness swept over Nosim. The familiar sights and smells of the village beckoned her. She longed to see her friend, Lilapa. Mother said that her young sister was sick. Milk was plentiful at this season. Even better than ugali was the cold, smoky sour milk waiting for her in the gourds at home. Also, her mother assured her, there was no intention of initiating her these holidays. 'Just come home,' her mother pleaded, 'and see us all, and when the holidays are over you can come back to school.' So Nosim went home.

# The Words of the New World

On her arrival at home she found her father very displeased with her. He had heard of her baptism. Why had she gone into the water like a cow being dipped? Was not the name her grandmother had chosen for her good enough? Had she forgotten she was a Maasai? Did she think she was a white girl or a Kikuyu? Did she despise her home? Did she not love her mother or respect her father any more? When she tried to explain, he got angry. Truly the medicine of the witch-doctor had not worked. She had been in school too long. She was being spoilt with all these new ideas. Certainly she was not to go back to school. He would have her prepared and married quickly, before the Chief could hear she was no longer in school.

The following day, when Nosim saw some irons being heated in the fire, she guessed they were for piercing her ear-lobes. She determined to run away. Quietly she stole into her mother's house and took a dress out of her box. She could not arrive back at school wearing the red-ochred cloth she had on. Quickly she changed and slipped out of the house. She crossed the enclosure and ran out of the gate, and no one had seen her. But there, right outside the gate, was her father tending some goats.

He came towards her angrily. 'Where are you going, you dressed-up schoolgirl?' he thundered at her. Then he grabbed her and beat her for the second time in her life; but this time with a stick, a stout staff he had in his hand, and it seemed to break every bone in her body. And the shame of it! Fathers do not beat their teenage daughters. He dragged her, sobbing, back into the village and to her mother.

'Here, take this girl of yours and look after her. The devil has got into her,' he said in disgusted tones and walked off.

She was in disgrace. No mercy was shown her now. Often only one ear at a time is pierced and the girl is petted and encouraged to bear the pain bravely. But on that fateful day Nosim was just grabbed roughly. The red-hot irons were jabbed ruthlessly through her ear-lobes and wooden plugs stuffed in the resulting holes. She sobbed on the cow-skin which was her bed and the blood from her ears mingled with her tears. But no one came to comfort her. Father was displeased with her so she was in disgrace with all. Pain and the rebellion in her heart kept her from sleeping.

Nor did the pain lessen as the days went by. Infection set in. Fresh, steaming cow-dung was plastered on the wound, that being the most readily available disinfectant her people had. How her ears and her whole body ached! She longed to take the wooden plugs out, but then the holes would close up and this torture would have to be endured all over again some other time. She knew that if only she could go to the hospital for an injection the infection would clear up quickly. But she dared not suggest it. Hospital was connected, in her father's mind, with school, modern ways, and the trend of change which must be resisted at all costs.

After many days of pain and fever the inflammation subsided and her ears healed. The plugs in the holes must be twisted round every day. Larger and still larger ones must be put in to prepare her ears for the day when she would wear the beaded leather strap which would show she was no longer a girl but a bride.

When the time came for her initiation, it was not the joyous time she had anticipated. Her heart was still rebellious. Her conscience nagged her about all the beer-drinking and dancing involved in the ceremony. She felt uncomfortable as she thought of how recently she had gone through the waters of baptism and now she was going through these heathen ceremonies. The worst of all was that she cried with pain and her mother was ashamed. This was proof that the ways of school spoilt girls and made them soft and cowardly.

Gradually she came to blame Jesus, the white people's God, for all her misery. She wished she had never been to school and heard about Him. She wished she had never been baptised and pretended to be a new person. She knew she was not changed; she was just the same as the other girls, in her heart. But they knew of no other way. There was turmoil in their hearts as there was in hers. The Jesus-way sounded so attractive when Ng'oto Ntoyie spoke of it at school. The Maasai way was so attractive to those right in it. But to Nosim, half in each world, it was all very confusing.

When the time of her initiation was over, preparations were started for her marriage. She had no say in the choice of her husband. Husbands were always arranged for daughters by their fathers. The girls always hoped they would be given someone they could respect.

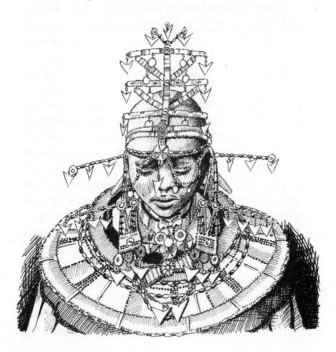

That was all they expected. Love was not something often found or even hoped for in Maasai marriages. She was very disappointed when she heard that the plan was for her to marry an old man. Only two of his other wives were still living. He was in the age-grade just senior to her father. Discussing this with Lilapa, they decided he would probably drink a lot, as old men usually do, but he would be too old to beat her very hard. The future did not look very attractive and Nosim's thoughts frequently turned back to school.

Often, as she sat sewing the ornaments she would wear for her marriage ceremony, she wondered what the girls at school were doing. Would they be in Maths class now? She did not mind missing that. But they might be training the choir for the Kenya Music Festival, or learning a new recipe in cooking class or having lots of fun in the playground after school. She thought it would be nice to be back at school with all her friends. She remembered all she had been taught about prayer. Ng'oto Ntoyie had told them that if they were in need Jesus would help them. But Nosim did not feel she had any right to pray to Jesus. She had only pretended to believe in Him. She wondered if there was any truth in what she had been taught at school. Her mother prayed to Enkai every morning, asking Him to care for them and keep them from sickness and danger. Nosim did not know if her mother ever wondered whether her god heard or bothered to answer her prayers. One day, while Nosim was out on the plains herding the calves, she decided to experiment. She would pray to God, the Father of Jesus, and ask Him to get her back to school. If He answered then it would be worthwhile being back because then she would know that the words about Jesus were true. If He did not answer, then she could be sure that the beliefs of the Europeans were not for her and her conscience could stop worrying her.

'O God, Father of Jesus, if You want me back at school to learn more about You, then somehow get me back to school soon.'

She felt quite light-hearted that evening as she took the calves home. The responsibility of choosing which way her life should go was taken off her young shoulders. God would have to act quickly if He was going to do anything, as the wedding ceremony was only three weeks off.

The very next day her father called her. The Chief was in the neighbouring village, just a mile or so away. He had received a letter on the bus the previous evening but neither he nor anyone else in the village could read. Someone had suggested Nosim.

Father, for a change, was rather proud that his daughter could do something that no one else in those two villages could do. They set off to obey the Chief's summons.

Father hoped in his heart that the Chief would not realise that Nosim had left school. Perhaps he would think it was holiday time or perhaps he would be so interested in his important letter that he would not think about the matter.

Nosim felt very important as her father took her to the Chief and she was introduced as the person who could read. The letter was handed to her and she glanced through it. It was from Ng'oto Ntoyie and it was about herself!

'Dear Chief,' she read silently to herself, 'In your section lives a girl called Ruth Nosim enole Kanka. She has not returned to school and is already five weeks late for this term. Could you kindly find out where she is and do all you can to

return her to school?' She read this with wonder. Can God answer prayers so quickly? She was surprised too that Ng'oto Ntoyie would go to the trouble of trying to find out where she was and want her back. If Ng'oto Ntoyie really loved her so much and if God could answer prayer so quickly, she suddenly wanted with all her heart to be back at school. What a pity Ng'oto Ntoyie had not worded the letter more strongly. Her father might be able to talk the Chief round.

'Come on, Girl,' broke in the Chief's voice. 'Can't you read it?'

'Yes, O Chief,' she said hesitantly, looking uncomfortably at Father. 'It says this: "In your section lives a girl called Nosim ene Kanka" – that's me,' she interjected. 'She still has not returned to school and is already five weeks late for this term. Could you kindly find out where she is and do all you can to return her to school?' Feeling that this appeal of her teacher's was far too weak, she added in desperation, 'And she says that if my father does not send me back to school immediately she will put him in jail!'

The Chief looked amused and Father looked uncomfortable. It was obvious to the Chief that the last part was Nosim's own addition. Here was a girl who wanted to return to school and whose father was preventing her. Officially the Chief was on the side of education and progress; the government paid him for just that purpose. Often, however, a chief could be persuaded, with the aid of a beer-drink and the offer of a fat ox, that a child had had enough education. But this time the Chief chose to side with the girl. He admired her courage and initiative in adding that bit about Ng'oto Ntoyie putting Father in jail. He also enjoyed seeing Father looking so uncomfortable. Within a few moments it was all arranged. Nosim was to go back to school the very next day on the bus. The Chief's own askari (policeman) was to accompany her to make sure Father did not try to prevent her. The Chief ordered Father to cancel the wedding arrangements and to return the cows already received as her dowry. He also told Father that Nosim still had many years of education ahead of her and that he had better start looking for a young educated man for Nosim to marry.

They walked back to the village in silence. Father was angry but powerless. Nosim was excited but also filled with a quiet wonder that the Great God, Father of Jesus, who controlled the sun and all the world, had heard her prayer. While she was praying the day before, the letter was already on the bus, coming to the Chief. What was the verse she had learned at school long ago? 'Before they call I will answer.' So the words of school were true after all!

# Right into the New World

Nosim went back to school with her heart wide open to all she could learn. Ng'oto Ntoyie hadn't deceived her. God did answer prayer. Nearly half the term had passed, by the time she arrived, and she had to work very hard to catch up. No more playing in class. There was point to all this learning at last. With the Chief helping her, she could go on with her education. Maybe she could even be a teacher herself one day, or a nurse, or write on a typewriter in an office.

One afternoon, during the Bible Lesson, Ng'oto Ntoyie was explaining to their class what being 'born again' meant. A hand went up at the back of the class. 'Please teacher,' asked the girl, 'tell us how you were born again.'

In the silence of the hot afternoon they settled down to listen to the story of a little girl in a far away country who attended beach services and heard of Jesus. How she had seen a picture of God's Son on the Cross and was told it was for her that He had died. They heard how she had knelt beside her bed that night, in the dark, and talked to Jesus. How she had said 'thank you' to Him and opened her heart for Him to come in.

'Now, some of you tell us how you found the Saviour,' challenged Ng'oto Ntoyie when she had finished.

Quickly Perisi jumped up and told of the day her teacher in the little bush school she had attended, had spoken to her. They had just finished the Bible Lesson and the rest of the children were going out for break. Perisi was cleaning the blackboard. 'Have you accepted Jesus as your Saviour, Perisi, or would you like to today?'

'I would love to, if you tell me how,' Perisi answered readily. The two of them had knelt right there next to the teacher's table and Perisi, still with the blackboard duster in her hand, had invited Jesus to be her Saviour.

Several other girls shared their experiences, and then Nainoi stood up. 'Because my father is a Christian,' she said, 'I thought I was too. But I see today that I have been pretending...' and she started sobbing.

It was nearly time for the bell so Ng'oto Ntoyie dismissed the class. 'If Jesus is talking to you,' she said, 'go off somewhere in the grounds by yourself and listen to Him, and give Him your answer.'

Nosim went outside in quiet wonder. She felt she was about to take the most important step in her life. She walked thoughtfully round behind the school vegetable garden, where she and her friends had so often stolen little carrots and green tomatoes. She sat down alone in the long grass and lifted her face to the sky.

'Oh God!' she breathed. 'When I talked to You, You listened and answered me. You talk to me now, and I'll answer.'

She quietly bowed her head and waited. She heard nothing but the quiet rustle of the grass. She felt nothing but the warm sun caressing the back of her neck. 'Him that cometh unto me I will in no wise cast out.' Quietly into her mind came a verse learned long ago in Sunday School. But it didn't sound, now, like a verse learned – it was Jesus Himself inviting her, Nosim, to come.

'Jesus, I am coming now, coming to You. Ng'oto Ntoyie told me long ago that I should come to You to let You change me. Here I am.

You have promised You won't cast me out. Please come in and change me.' She remembered how quickly God had answered her prayer before. He always answers. 'Thank you, Jesus. I know you have answered,' she breathed. And into her heart stole a peace and joy that warmed her heart as the sun was warming her body. It was a long time before she wanted to move. Jesus was there and she wanted to stay with her new Friend. 'I am with you always,' her new Friend reminded her.

Nosim got up and wandered back to the classroom. A playmate called her to join in a game of dodge-ball, but she just waved to her. She would have to tell Ng'oto Ntoyie what she had just done but she felt a little shy. She peeped in at the classroom window and saw that her teacher was still there. She was talking to three of her classmates. Nosim opened the door and went in quietly.

'Come in, Nosim,' called out Ng'oto Ntoyie. 'Do you want to accept Jesus as your Saviour also?'

'No,' said Nosim. 'I just wanted to tell you that I have! Out there behind the garden. I have asked Him to come in and change me, like you told me long ago.'

# Struggles of the New World

The days that followed were happy ones. Several of Nosim's friends were also real Christians now. Some of her old friends dropped her when they saw she didn't want to join in with the old ways any more. But that didn't hurt much. She loved to go off with Perisi and some other girls who also loved Jesus and they prayed together and shared lovely things they were discovering in God's Book. But her favourite times were early in the morning, after the matron had woken up the girls in the dormitories. She would wrap herself up in a blanket, for it is cold in the early mornings on the highlands of Kenya, take her Bible and go and huddle next to a classroom or in her precious spot behind the garden, and talk to her new Master.

Nosim had to work very hard in school now. In a couple of months she would be writing the examinations which would bring to an end the time at the Mission school. She had missed a lot of work when she was away, and even before that, she had not studied very well. School had seemed so pointless. Back in her village she would not need all the Science and Mathematics and other hard subjects. Now all was different.

She was anxious to learn. Rising in her heart was a timid desire to be a teacher. Dare she pray about it? To be a teacher she would have to pass the examination – and not very many managed that. To be a teacher she would have to go to College for two years, and would Father agree to that? There would be fees and clothes and many things needed and her family wouldn't understand.

One Friday morning they were to write a Geography test and Nosim wasn't ready. There was so much to study and the facts just would not stay in her head. When she went off that morning she took her Geography book instead of her Bible and she studied instead of praying.

'Wasn't the Scripture Union Bible Reading lovely this morning?' Perisi whispered as they lined up outside the dining hall before breakfast.

Nosim turned on a vague smile. 'Yes, it was very interesting.' And quickly turned to talk to another girl. She felt miserable and avoided Perisi as they finished breakfast and went to the classroom. The test was written up on the blackboard and Nosim panicked. She didn't know anything. She longed to bow her head and cry to her Friend, Jesus to help her, but she felt she had no right to do so. She had neglected Him, she had deceived the other girls, she had lied to Perisi. She struggled on with the test, heavy hearted and miserable. Now she would never become a teacher; she would fail. She could not now pray to Jesus to change Father's heart on the matter. She probably didn't even belong to Him. Her heart was still wicked and she wasn't changed after all. She was one of the last to hand in her paper, as she sat for a long time to think of elusive answers.

'What is the matter, Nosim?' whispered Ng'oto Ntoyie as she eventually took her paper up and hid it under the pile.

'Nothing,' snapped Nosim rudely and turned her face away.

But at break time Nosim didn't want to see her friends so she took her Bible and went to her favourite place. Perhaps, just perhaps Jesus would still talk to her from His Word. With all the misery that comes from a heart disappointed with oneself and cut off from the One best loved, she turned to the Scripture Union portion for the day.

'If we confess our sins He is faithful and just to forgive us our sins and to cleanse us...' Soon her confession was flowing as freely as her tears and she knew she was forgiven, cleansed, restored.

It was a radiant Nosim who went back to class and Ng'oto Ntoyie, seeing the change, lifted her heart in praise. It had been worth spending break time praying for Nosim when it was so obvious that a victory had been won.

When the time came for the big examination, Nosim felt a little more prepared. But her trust was not in herself. Her new Master had spoken to her from His Book. 'If anyone lack wisdom let him ask and it shall be given.' She was sadly lacking, but she had asked and trusted it would be given. She even had hopes for the future. There were such precious promises in God's book. 'Be delighted with the Lord. Then He will give you all your heart's desires. Commit everything you do to the Lord. Trust Him to help you do it, and He will!'

The examinations over, they were soon busy with the Christmas programme which they were to put on for the parents who came to the prize-giving in the last week of the school year.

The play that Nosim acted in spoke to her heart. After the choir had sung a song about searching for God, Nosim and three other girls who were 'seekers,' went to a Rich Man, to a Wise Man and to an Old Man, but none of them could say that they had found the way to God. Then the fourth seeker found in the Word of God that Jesus was the Way and they went to worship, with the Shepherds, at the manger of the Christ child. The choir then sang 'Go tell it to your neighbour in darkness here below,' and Nosim stood up and said, 'Now that we have found the Way, we should go and tell our neighbours.' This was followed by a scene where the four schoolgirls, with big Bible pictures, of the Christmas story,

arrived at a Maasai village to share the message
with them. The scene ended with the Maasai man
and woman and the girls kneeling at the manger,
singing 'Oh come let us adore Him, Christ, the
Lord.' Every time they practised the play, and
especially on the great day, when they acted it
before a crowded audience of parents and other
visitors, the scene spoke to Nosim's heart. 'Now
that I have found the Way, I should go and tell
the people my village.' And her heart ached for
the day when her mother and father, brothers
and sisters too would kneel and worship Jesus.

The farewell party that Nosim's class held
on the last afternoon of the term was an
unforgettable memory for the girls. Teachers
whom they had thought so grown-up and wise
joined them in a riot of party games. It was fun
watching the Maths and History teachers wildly
waving paper frogs the length of the school
dining-room. Nosim felt sad that so soon she
would be leaving the school that had been home
for so many months of the year. But there was
still something she wanted to ask Ng'oto Ntoyie.
She waited around when the party was over, for
a chance to speak to her.

'Can you help me?' asked Nosim when she
got her attention. 'I would like to tell the people
of my village about Jesus, like we did in the play,
but I don't know how.'

Ng'oto Ntoyie's heart sang for joy. She took
Nosim to her house and gave her some pictures;
she suggested which choruses to teach the
children and then patiently showed the excited

Nosim how to work a little Gospel Recordings record-player – how to turn the handle at just the right speed and how to change the needle.

'You show by being loving and helpful, Nosim, that you are different. Then they will all want to hear these words.'

And so when the school year closed Nosim left for the last time. Excited to be going home, sad to leave the Mission school which had become so much part of her life. But especially in her heart was a real desire to live for her new Friend and Master at home.

'Yes, Nosim,' called out Ng'oto Ntoyie as the bus-driver climbed in and the excited girls were about to set off home, 'if you pass I will come and talk to your father and we'll see what you can do next year. Remember, trust Him to help you and He will.'

# Her Two Worlds Meet

Could that be Ng'oto Ntoyie's car she heard? Nosim was a little way from home, caring for the calves. No car had ever come to their village before as it was several miles from the road. But there, picking its way carefully between the thorn trees and scratching its way through the bushes, came the red Kombi the schoolgirls loved to ride in.

Instead of running to welcome her teacher, she fled in the opposite direction. She could not possible receive Ng'oto Ntoyie dressed as she was! With the nearest waterhole miles away, it was very hard to keep clean. So, afraid to spoil the few pretty dresses she had, she had put on the old ochred cloths that never needed washing.

The car drove up to the gateway and all the little children fled. What strange monster was this? The women, a little bolder, clutched their babies tightly and went nearer.

'Oh! It is only Ng'oto Ntoyie,' one exclaimed. The others quickly gathered round to greet this strange person they had heard about, who spoke their language but looked so different.

'Come and greet Ng'oto Ntoyie,' the mothers called to their children who had run off and were now peeping through the gateway. 'She gives sweets to children,' added the woman who had first recognised her, having met her when she was preaching in another area. The bolder ones edged forward and came as near as they dared, to present their heads for a greeting, and then scampered back to the safety of mother's cloth. Others thought the risk too great, even for a sweet.

Nosim came hurrying across the muddy cattle enclosure, still tying the belt of her dress. Proudly she introduced her teacher to her father and mother and her little sister and then took her visitor to her mother's house. 'My teacher is a very queer person,' she whispered to her mother, as they went. 'She prefers tea to our lovely smoked sour milk.' So quickly the embers were blown up to a flame and a pot of water was put on the crackling fire.

'Would you like your daughter to continue with learning, Father of Nosim?' Ng'oto Ntoyie asked. Nosim's heart leapt. Had she passed? Had God really answered her prayers again?

'Hasn't she been reading for many years? Doesn't she know everything already?' protested Father. But he looked proudly at his daughter and Nosim's hopes grew.

'True, O Father of Nosim, she has been at school for many years but now she could go to

a Training College and become a teacher. Soon she could be earning money every month.'

His daughter earn money! The thought was surprising, but not altogether unpleasant. He would never let any of his children go and work for someone – become a servant, labourer. Only poor people did that! But to earn money being a teacher. That was not a disgrace, and it might be useful to have access to some shillings without having to sell one of his precious cows.

'Have I passed?' Nosim asked excitedly, not able to contain the question any longer.

'Yes, Nosim, you have passed and the Education Officer has places for six of you in Teacher Training. Would you like to go?'

Would she! Her eyes shining with excitement, she pleaded with her father.

'Just two years,' she explained, 'at that school and then I'll be a Mwalimu. I can come and teach at Oltinka School,' she planned, indicating the little bush school at the nearby trading centre; 'then I can come home often.'

Father felt pleased with himself. He had been against this thing called school for many years. Now it seemed that it was of use after all. He opened his blanket and spat on his chest in self-congratulation. A girl of his could learn and write tests and pass and become a Mwalimu and earn shillings! He thought of the cows he would get as a dowry when Nosim married. This teaching would delay that. Perhaps the old man with whom he was making arrangements would not want to wait much longer.

'But she is going to get married soon,' protested Father.

'Menye Nosim,' suggested Ng'oto Ntoyie from her long experience, 'let your daughter become a teacher and then arrange for her marriage to an educated man and he will give you more cows for her.'

Nosim's mother did not look pleased about all this conversation but it was of no use to protest. Fathers, not mothers, owned the children. Anyway, she loved Nosim dearly and it was plain to see that she had set her heart on becoming a teacher.

'She will need money for fees and she will need more clothes if she is going to a College in the big city of Nairobi,' explained Ng'oto Ntoyie.

She already had a box of clothes; there were two, or maybe even three dresses in it. These people of the new ways seemed to change their clothes so often and need so many things. But Nosim's father was a proud man. His daughter must hold up her head in the city.

'I will sell a cow next week at the cattle auction and send you 200 shillings,' he promised.

So Nosim's prayers were answered – and while Ng'oto Ntoyie sipped her outsize mug of tea, the excited girl chatted happily to her about the things she would need and all the thrilling details of the life opening out before her.

That business over, they gathered the people of the village under a shady tree outside the enclosure. Ng'oto Ntoyie got her record-player out – it was easier to work than the little one she had given Nosim. One didn't have to turn a handle. As she took the records out, one woman spoke.

'Have you the same plates as this girl?' she asked. 'She has played them to us often. We like the one of the sheep that got lost, best. They are good words.'

153

With a song of praise in her heart, Ng'oto Ntoyie played the record of the Lost Sheep while she sorted her pictures. Nosim had witnessed faithfully and prepared the way, and now her village wanted to hear more of these good words. And so another village heard of the Shepherd who had come to seek the Lost and of the price he had paid to save them.

'The children know some choruses,' said Nosim proudly.

Even the little toddlers, clad only in a string of beads, clapped as enthusiastically as the children, and heartily, if not tunefully, sang the songs Nosim had taught them. Ng'oto Ntoyie gave out sweets as a reward and while Nosim

went to the house to get the box with her few possessions, the children, who had at first been so afraid, clambered in and out of the 'big red monster' and chatted happily to the strange white woman.

Nosim kissed her tearful mother goodbye, listened respectfully as Father gave her instructions about the money he would send, then she climbed in beside Ng'oto Ntoyie and off they drove, off to a new and wonderful future.

Several miles later she wondered vaguely if anyone would remember the calves she was supposed to be looking after. But all the thoughts of going to College soon drowned her conscience and she settled down to enjoy her dreams.

# Equipped for the New World

A dozen handkerchiefs! Why, Nosim had never owned more than one, and now she was to have a dozen all at once.

'You must pay 100 shillings fee when you arrive at College,' explained Ng'oto Ntoyie. 'That will leave you 100 shillings to spend.' It seemed a vast sum of money to Nosim but when they were at the counter of the local shop it dwindled away alarmingly. A red cardigan, a suitcase for her things, a pair of brown shoes, a raincoat, a pair of scissors ... the money was finished long before they got to such items as sheets and two white blouses for Physical Education. So, many yards of white cloth was bought and Nosim proudly made her own blouses – with teacher's help of course. As she hemmed sheets she wondered about them. She had never used sheets before. They just slept under a cheap cotton blanket at school. Truly, sleeping in sheets made her almost a teacher already. It was only when she arrived at College that she discovered that one didn't put all three sheets on one's bed at once!

Another item of wonder on the list of things required was toothpaste and a brush. Fancy having to spend money on cleaning her teeth when always she had just chewed a little stick and used that. She supposed there were no trees in the City and that was why the people bought brushes.

But there were many more lovely surprises for Nosim. Kind ladies in far-off countries had knitted warm jerseys and made pretty dresses and had sent them to Ng'oto Ntoyie for just such a need as this. So dresses were tried on and altered, skirts were matched up with pretty blouses and folded away carefully in the new suitcase.

A prized possession was a brand new Bible with Scripture Union notes tucked away inside, which her teacher had given her. She was a bit bewildered by Ng'oto Ntoyie's warnings. Were not all white people Christians? All those she had met were. Yet she was warned that she might meet people at her College in the City who would tell her that it was old fashioned to believe in Jesus and that the Bible was an old out-of-date book no one believed in any more!

Out of date! Hadn't she just, this past week, seen God keep a promise from that book? Old-fashioned to believe in Jesus! No, her family and all the dear ones out in the villages still followed the old fashion – the old life of darkness and groping after their god. This knowing Jesus was new and wonderful and real.

And so the girl of two worlds set off on her great adventure. She still loved her old world dearly. The old life of cattle and the wide plains, of smoked milk and red-ochred cloths, of

belonging in the village and the warm security of familiar things.

She loved too the new world she was tasting – the world of books and pencils, of pretty dresses and soap, the excitement of the city and the interest of new things.

Out in the new world, back in the old – she had Jesus with her and that was what mattered.

A poised young lady stepped up into the bus and it quickly disappeared in a cloud of dust on its way to the City. Could it be the little girl who, a few short years ago, had cried in terror as she set off to school for the first time?

# Who are the Maasai?

## THE MAASAI – Then and Now.

The Maasai are a proud cattle people who live in the south of Kenya and across the border into Tanzania, where the great Game Parks are. The Maasai consider the game to be God's cattle and so they can live at peace with wild animals, in gratitude for giving them, the Maasai, all the cattle in the world. But lions are the exception! Every young warrior must have taken part in a successful lion hunt to be considered a man. Being so proud of their own culture they have not hungered after western ways and education like other Africans have. They believe in a Creator God who loves them (only) They don't worship ancestors like most Africans do because they don't believe there is life after death. They always enjoy hearing of heaven, of God sending his Son to be their 'olkipoket' – sin-offering but many don't want to believe because many changes in behaviour would have to be made if they truly came to Jesus.

But these days there are many Maasai Christians. The educated ones go to churches like ours, as they are part of modern Kenya. Those who are still part of the cattle-village life, worship in meeting places in the shade of a tree, or in a little corrugated-iron building. They sing songs in their own kind of music, with clapping and dancing, songs that they make up as they praise the God they know in truth in Jesus. The educated Maasai have changed, either in jobs or professions, or have ranches with beef cattle and are prosperous, except when drought devastates all cattle people. Others carry on their old ways except where government pressures squeeze them to conform.

The girls you read about in the book went on to be teachers, nurses, and secretaries in modern Kenya. One is the first Maasai lady doctor. Another brought her children up in Japan, as the wife of Kenya's ambassador to that fascinating land. But generally the Maasai fathers still try to force their daughters into early marriages. These days there are girls who have gone on to High Schools, Colleges and even University who don't go home for the holidays, but go back to their old school where it all started, where there is a hostel for them to stay undisturbed to continue their education, and not have to submit to an arranged marriage and the initiation rites.

# *Africa Inland Mission*

AIM was founded over 100 years ago when the young Peter Cameron Scott, a man with a clear vision, gathered around him a group of fellow workers. Cameron Scott records that he '...seemed to see a line of mission stations stretching from the coast, on into the mysteries of the Sahara Desert.'

The small group that arrived in Mombasa in 1895 made their way inland. It was not long before disease overtook them and before two years was up, all but one of them had died. Scott himself died of blackwater fever. But all was not lost. The survivor stayed on and before long others joined him. Over the years the work has spread, initially from Kenya out to Tanzania, Congo, Uganda and Central Africa Republic. Just as all these countries have found political independence, so the churches planted by AIM have taken on their independence, so that AIM's role is now largely that of a support to these churches.

During the 1970s AIM entered a new phase in which we began research into countries where we had not previously been involved. In a number of them, this led to starting work with already established churches and assisting them in outreach to new areas. AIM also works among Africans in the United States, UK and in Romania. AIM currently has 750 members from 15 or so different nationalities, most of whom are working in Africa.

In all new endeavours we are looking for partnership with national churches and other mission agencies developing leadership in all sectors of African life. We are presently researching new openings in parts of Africa where we have not previously worked.

Alongside those involved directly in these ministries we also have administrators, accountants, pilots and aircraft mechanics, and teachers for the children of missionaries.

Contact details:

AIM International
3 Halifax Place
Nottingham
NG1 1QN

www.aimint.org/eu

# Pray for Africa and the Maasai

Remarkable changes have taken place in Africa over the past twenty or thirty years, but there are underlying concerns that do not appear to be responding to the best endeavours of national and world leaders. Patrick Johnstone in Operation World outlines five trends to watch. For us, these are matters for prayer.

- **AIDS** continues to place a heavy toll on the continent. Weak democratic governments and institutions with resulting civil unrest and outright war should motivate us to pray for Christian leaders in all areas of government and society.

- **Tension** between Christian and Muslim populations is particularly evident along the 'line' which extends from Senegal across the Sahel to Ethiopia. These tensions sometimes erupt in violence as seen in Nigeria.

- **Deepening poverty.** Africa's share of world trade is decreasing, its people are becoming poorer and trained professionals are not staying to practise in their native countries. Some debt relief has been agreed but many counties are still burdened by debt repayment.

- **Traditions.** Despite enormous growth in the church during the past one hundred years, traditional African religions still command wide influence. It may not be possible to fully understand some of the continent's problems without taking this into account.

- **Maasai Children.** That the many Maasai children, and the millions of children throughout Africa, will come to know Jesus as their Saviour while they are young. That they will change to become new people inside, not just change to western ways and clothes.

- **Education.** That Maasai children, and the many others, who want education, choice of careers and marriage partners, may have the opportunity and will use their freedom wisely.

- **Abuse.** Maasai children are usually loved and valued, but many children in Africa are abused, abandoned and exploited. Pray for protection by loving adults of all children.

- **Orphans.** That Africa's children who are being orphaned and are suffering through aids and war will receive the home-care, health-care and the love they should have.

- **Missionaries.** That God would bless the missionaries and aid organizations with safety and all they need to help Africa's children. That help will reach the really needy, that none will be left out.

- **Me and You.** That God would show each of us who read this what our part could be in helping Africa's vulnerable children, in prayer, giving and sending help - and even going ourselves.

# Map of Africa

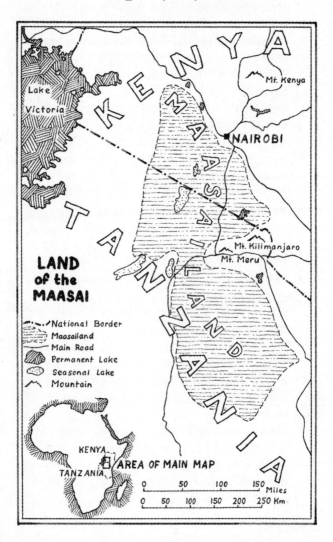

KENYA

Lake Victoria

Mt. Kenya

MAASAI

■ NAIROBI

TANZANIA

LAND of the MAASAI

Mt. Kilimanjaro
Mt. Meru

National Border
Maasailand
Main Road
Permanent Lake
Seasonal Lake
Mountain

TANZANIA

KENYA
TANZANIA

AREA OF MAIN MAP

| 0 | 50 | 100 | 150 Miles |
| 0 | 50 | 100 | 150 | 200 | 250 Km |

# About the Author

Lorna Eglin, born in Cape Town, South Africa, was a missionary with AIM International in Kenya for forty-five years. She, together with her missionary colleague, Betty Allcock, are happily retired in South Africa. They are still in touch with many Kenya friends and are pushing 'missions' in their local church. Lorna is still writing – currently about the adventures they had as they worked with the proud cattle-people, the Maasai and other Maasai-speaking groups.

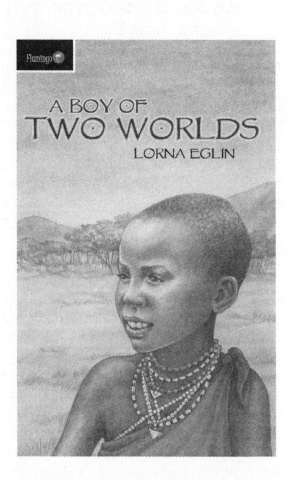

A BOY OF
TWO WORLDS

LORNA EGLIN

ISBN: 978-1-84550-126-6

# A Boy of Two Worlds
## by Lorna Eglin

Maasai boys love to practice throwing spears, and jumping. One day they will be strong men and leaders of their tribe. Lemayan is excellent with the goats and his father is proud of his capable son. One dreadful day all that changes and the tribe's way of life hangs in the balance; the drought attacks their pastures; worms attack the cattle and the whole tribe has to sell all their animals. To make matters worse Lemayan falls sick - but no one realises just how sick. Lemayan only knows the traditional Maasai world... but now he has to live in a different world. What will that different world offer him? Will he be happy? Will anything be as good as looking after animals? When Lemayan finds out about a Good Shepherd who cares for his sheep he begins another journey of discovery... a journey to yet another world ... a world where the Jesus is King... and where all tribes and peoples are welcome.

## The Adventures Series
### An ideal series to collect

Have you ever wanted to visit the rainforest? Have you ever longed to sail down the Amazon River? Would you just love to go on safari in Africa? Well these books can help you imagine that you are actually there.

Pioneer missionaries retell their amazing adventures and encounters with animals and nature. In the Amazon you will discover tree frogs, piranha fish and electric eels. In the Rainforest you will be amazed at the armadillo and the toucan. In the blistering heat of the African Savannah you will come across lions and elephants and hyenas. And you will discover how God is at work in these amazing environments.

ISBN: 978-1-85792-807-5

African Adventures by Dick Anderson
ISBN 978-1-85792-807-5
Amazon Adventures by Horace Banner
ISBN 978-1-85792-440-4
Antarctic Adventures by Bartha Hill
ISBN 978-1-78191-135-8
Cambodian Adventures by Donna Vann
ISBN 978-1-84550-474-8
Emerald Isle Adventures by Robert Plant
ISBN 978-1-78191-136-5
Great Barrier Reef Adventures by Jim Cromarty
ISBN 978-1-84550-068-9
Himalayan Adventures by Penny Reeve
ISBN 978-1-84550-080-1
Kiwi Adventures by Bartha Hill
ISBN 978-1-84550-282-9
New York City Adventures by Donna Vann
ISBN 978-1-84550-546-2
Outback Adventures by Jim Cromarty
ISBN 978-1-85792-974-4
Pacific Adventures by Jim Cromarty
ISBN 978-1-84550-475-5
Rainforest Adventures by Horace Banner
ISBN 978-1-85792-627-9
Rocky Mountain Adventures by Betty Swinford
ISBN 978-1-85792-962-1
Scottish Highland Adventures by
Catherine Mackenzie
ISBN 978-1-84550-281-2
Wild West Adventures by Donna Vann
ISBN 978-1-84550-065-8

# TRAILBLAZER SERIES

# Start collecting this series now!

### Ten Boys who used their Talents:
ISBN 978-1-84550-146-4
Paul Brand, Ghillean Prance, C.S.Lewis,
C.T. Studd, Wilfred Grenfell, J.S. Bach,
James Clerk Maxwell, Samuel Morse,
George Washington Carver, John Bunyan.

### Ten Girls who used their Talents:
ISBN 978-1-84550-147-1
Helen Roseveare, Maureen McKenna,
Anne Lawson, Harriet Beecher Stowe,
Sarah Edwards, Selina Countess of Huntingdon,
Mildred Cable, Katie Ann MacKinnon,
Patricia St. John, Mary Verghese.

### Ten Boys who Changed the World:
ISBN 978-1-85792-579-1
David Livingstone, Billy Graham, Brother Andrew,
John Newton, William Carey, George Müller,
Nicky Cruz, Eric Liddell, Luis Palau,
Adoniram Judson.

### Ten Girls who Changed the World:
ISBN 978-1-85792-649-1
Corrie ten Boom, Mary Slessor,
Joni Eareckson Tada, Isobel Kuhn,
Amy Carmichael, Elizabeth Fry, Evelyn Brand,
Gladys Aylward, Catherine Booth, Jackie Pullinger.

### Ten Boys who Made a Difference:
ISBN 978-1-85792-775-7
Augustine of Hippo, Jan Hus, Martin Luther,
Ulrich Zwingli, William Tyndale, Hugh Latimer,
John Calvin, John Knox, Lord Shaftesbury,
Thomas Chalmers.

**Ten Girls who Made a Difference**:
ISBN 978-1-85792-776-4
Monica of Thagaste, Catherine Luther,
Susanna Wesley, Ann Judson, Maria Taylor,
Susannah Spurgeon, Bethan Lloyd-Jones,
Edith Schaeffer, Sabina Wurmbrand,
Ruth Bell Graham.

**Ten Boys who Made History**:
ISBN 978-1-85792-836-5
Charles Spurgeon, Jonathan Edwards,
Samuel Rutherford, D L Moody,
Martin Lloyd Jones, A W Tozer, John Owen,
Robert Murray McCheyne, Billy Sunday,
George Whitfield.

**Ten Girls who Made History**:
ISBN 978-1-85792-837-2
Ida Scudder, Betty Green, Jeanette Li,
Mary Jane Kinnaird, Bessie Adams,
Emma Dryer, Lottie Moon, Florence Nightingale,
Henrietta Mears, Elisabeth Elliot.

**Ten Boys who Didn't Give In:**
ISBN 978-1-84550-035-1
Polycarp, Alban, Sir John Oldcastle
Thomas Cranmer, George Wishart,
James Chalmers, Dietrich Bonhoeffer,
Nate Saint, Ivan Moiseyev,
Graham Staines.

**Ten Girls who Didn't Give In:**
ISBN 978-1-84550-036-8
Blandina, Perpetua, Lady Jane Grey,
Anne Askew, Lysken Dirks, Marion Harvey,
Margaret Wilson, Judith Weinberg,
Betty Stam, Esther John.

CHRISTIAN FOCUS PUBLICATIONS

Christian Focus | Christian Heritage | CF4K | Mentor

Christian Focus Publications publishes books for adults and children under its four main imprints: Christian Focus, CF4K, Mentor and Christian Heritage. Our books reflect our conviction that God's Word is reliable and Jesus is the way to know him, and live for ever with him.

Our children's publication list includes a Sunday School curriculum that covers pre-school to early teens, and puzzle and activity books. We also publish personal and family devotional titles, biographies and inspirational stories that children will love.

If you are looking for quality Bible teaching for children then we have an excellent range of Bible stories and age-specific theological books.

From pre-school board books to teenage apologetics, we have it covered!

# Find us at our web page:
# www.christianfocus.com

CF4·K
Because you're never
too young to know Jesus